FEAR

DIRK KURBJUWEIT

Translated from the German by Imogen Taylor

ORION

First published in Great Britain in 2018 by Orion Books,
an imprint of The Orion Publishing Group Ltd
Carmelite House, 50 Victoria Embankment,
London EC4Y 0DZ

An Hachette UK company

1 3 5 7 9 10 8 6 4 2

First published in German as *Angst* by Rowohlt Berlin Verlag GmbH Berlin in 2013
Copyright © Dirk Kurbjuweit 2013
First published in English in Australia by Text Publishing Pty Limited in 2017

The moral right of Dirk Kurbjuweit to be identified as
the author of this work has been asserted in accordance with
the Copyright, Designs and Patents Act of 1988.

A CIP catalogue record for this book is
available from the British Library.

ISBN (Hardback) 978 1 4091 7202 4
ISBN (Export Trade Paperback) 978 1 4091 7588 9

Printed and bound by CPI Group (UK) Ltd, Croydon, CR0 4YY

MIX
Paper from
responsible sources
FSC
www.fsc.org
FSC® C104740

www.orionbooks.co.uk

For my children

1

'DAD?'

My father didn't answer me. He barely speaks anymore. He isn't muddled, doesn't suffer from dementia or Alzheimer's. We know that, because he does speak sometimes, and on those rare occasions he is lucid and rational. Dad is seventy-eight, but his memories haven't abandoned him, and he always recognises me when I visit him. I get a smile, not a big one, because that's the way he is—distant, reserved—but he recognises me, and he's pleased I come to see him. That is no small thing.

'Mr Tiefenthaler?' Kottke prompted, when my father didn't reply. Sometimes my father is more likely to respond to Kottke than to me. Does that make me jealous? I have to admit that it does a bit. On the other hand, Kottke is the man my father now spends his days with, and I'm glad—of course I am—that they get on. Kottke respects my father—I think it's fair to say that. I don't know whether he treats all the men here as gently and kindly as he treats Dad. I suspect that he doesn't, although I have never seen him with the other men.

But today my father didn't respond to Kottke either. He sat at the table in silence, half asleep, eyes drooping, hands hanging by his sides. Every now and then he would tilt forwards and I would get a fright, because if my father hit his face on the metal tabletop he would hurt himself. He never falls that far, though—he always checks the tilting movement and rights himself. It was the same today, but I can't get used to it. It gives me a fright every time. I saw Kottke start forward and then relax—he too had been ready to intervene. We take good care that nothing happens to Dad.

I've been coming to visit my father in this place for six months, and it's still sad to see him like this, in his threadbare shirt and the worn trousers he wears without a belt. We bought him new things to smarten him up, but he insists on wearing his old familiar clothes, and why shouldn't he? He looks strange, sitting there, because his chair is too far from the table—as is mine. We sit opposite each other, but the table doesn't really connect us, doesn't allow us to sit together. Now, of all times, when we're closer than ever before, the table separates us. At least that's the way I see it. Unfortunately it's not possible to move the chairs, because they're screwed to the floor. The same goes for the table.

My father could speak if he wanted to, but he doesn't. He's tired, I think, worn out by the long life he found so difficult. We never understood him, but what does that matter? He had to cope with those difficulties, even if he maybe only imagined them. And we don't know everything about his life. Nobody knows everything about another person's life. We can only be continuously present in our own lives, and even that doesn't mean we know all about them, because things that affect us—often momentous things—can happen without our being there, and even without our knowledge. So we should be wary of making statements about other's lives in their entirety. I am.

As I was leaving the house this morning, I told my wife I was going to drop in on my father. I always put it like that, and when she goes, she uses the same phrase: 'I'll drop in on your father later.' Half a year is not enough to take the pain out of the word 'prison', not for people like us, who must first get used to the idea that such a place has become part of our world. It hurts us, even now.

My father was sentenced at the age of seventy-seven and has already had—I won't say celebrated—one birthday as an inmate. We tried to make the hour's visit festive, but it was not a success. It wasn't so much the screwed-down chairs and metal table that were to blame, or even the barred window—another all-too-clear reminder that this was not a homey place, not a fitting place to celebrate the fact of your own birth. It was me.

We had carried off the first half-hour fairly well. We all sang 'Happy Birthday to You'—my wife, Rebecca, and I; our children, Paul and Fay; my mother; and even Kottke, who had granted us certain exemptions that day. We ate the almond cake my mother has been baking for her husband almost all her life, and which she wanted to present uncut on a baking sheet the way she always does, because she enjoys cutting it with everyone looking on, waiting to have some. But the exemptions didn't go that far. When we were searched at the door, my poor mother, my seventy-five-year-old mother, had to watch as a prison warder cut her almond cake into little pieces. 'I assure you I didn't bake a file into it,' she said, with a forced cheerfulness that made me sad. They probably believed her, but of course there are rules. I hate those words, hate having it pointed out to me that there are rules preventing what is reasonable. But they are words I have heard often since my father has been in prison.

We talked about other birthdays—birthdays my father had celebrated as a free man—when I suddenly found myself sobbing, quite unexpectedly. At first I thought I could stop and I fought back the sobs, but they grew heavier until I was weeping uncontrollably. My children had never seen their father in such a state and stared at me in horror. Kottke, bless him, looked away, embarrassed. My mother, who was sitting on one of the screwed-down chairs, stood up and came towards me, but my wife reached me first. She took me in her arms, and I buried my face in her shoulder. After a few minutes my sobbing fit was over, and I looked up. My eyes still blurred with tears, I saw my father regarding me with what can only be described as interest—a peculiar interest I did not know how to interpret. I have often wondered about it since, but have come up with nothing that could explain that look. My mother passed me a paper napkin, and I apologised and began, quickly and far too cheerfully, to recount some story about another of my father's birthdays. But this time it was no more than an attempt to speed up the clock, because I wanted to get out. We all wanted to get out.

I shouldn't write that—it seems a bit much, when your father's in prison. If anyone had to get out, it was my father, but he couldn't. We, on the other hand, would be leaving as soon as possible, and as four o'clock approached, we transferred what was left of the cake from the baking sheet to two paper plates—one for my father and one for Kottke and his colleagues—and then we hugged him and left, not forgetting to say thank you to Kottke. My father remained behind, of course. He'd been sentenced to eight years. The six months he spent in remand count towards that, and he's served another six months here in Tegel, which leaves seven years. If he behaves well—and we firmly expect him to do so—he might be released in three or four years' time. Kottke has told us repeatedly that there is no better-behaved inmate than my father, and that fuels our hopes. It would give him another few good years of life as a free man. That's what I tell my mother. 'If only he doesn't die in there,' my mother often says, and immediately repeats herself: 'If only he doesn't die in there.'

'He's healthy,' I tell her, when she says that. 'He'll make it.'

'Dad?' I asked again, after chatting a while with Kottke. That's how I tend to spend my time here: Kottke and I talk. He does most of the talking—Kottke's nothing if not talkative—but that's a good thing. It's a help. I find the silence of the prison intolerable, because eerie sounds emanate from it that can be heard in the visitors' room—metallic noises I can't identify, not ringing out sharply, but flat and dull. At first I thought I could hear rhythms, as if somebody was tapping or filing, but over time I realised that I had become the victim of my own expectations—namely, that a prison must always be filled with the sounds of thwarted communication or attempted flight. There were no rhythms, nor was there any quiet sighing such as I once thought I heard—only unfamiliar, unaccountable noises coming from deep inside the building. I was glad when Kottke drowned out these sounds with his grating Berlin accent. He has a long career as a jailer behind him—more than forty years serving the law—and has a great many stories to tell. I never really wanted to know so much about the world of crime and criminals, but that world is not without interest, especially now that it intersects with our own.

Kottke was soon looking at the clock. He has an unerring instinct, always knowing when our hour together is up. 'Time we made a move,' he said, as usual, and I was grateful to him: this turn of phrase makes it sound as if the two of them have to leave a pleasant coffee party and drive home. Home for my father is a cell, but this uncomfortable fact is obscured by Kottke's well-chosen words. A jailer's sensitivity—there is such a thing. We've been lucky.

Until then, Kottke had been leaning against the wall next to the window. Hardly had he spoken when he took two steps across the room towards my father and put out a hand to touch his upper arm. He always does that—there are a whole host of rituals here, of repetitions and routines. In this place the gesture seems almost official, a warning that it's not worth trying to escape, because Kottke, friendly though he may be, must do his duty. But I think he acts out of solicitude—he wants to support my father, even though there's no need. Dad is quite capable of getting up by himself.

When Dad stood up, so did I. We gave each other a brief hug (we can now), and then he left, Kottke at his side. My father is taller than his guard: a slim six foot two to Kottke's corpulent five foot six. He is still as trim as ever, but he has lost his hair, and with age his legs have become bowed, giving him a rolling gait like a seaman. Not that he ever was a seaman—my father was a mechanic and then a car salesman.

When they had left, another jailer appeared, one whose name I don't know. He too was fat (a lot of the men here are), and he looked dutiful rather than friendly. We didn't exchange a single word as he accompanied me to the door. At last, the street—cars, birds, wind in the trees, life. Twenty paces off, my Audi winked cheerily when I pressed the button on my car key.

2

WHY IS MY FATHER IN PRISON? I don't have to make a big secret of it. He has been found guilty of manslaughter.

If he was sentenced to just eight years, that is because he confessed, and because his motives seemed less atrocious, somehow, than those of a murderer. We accepted the court's judgement. It is hard for us, but we can't say that justice has been ill served. My father agrees. Of course he had hoped for a mild sentence, but it was clear to him from the outset that he would go to jail as a result of his actions. There can be no talk of a spur-of-the-moment act—it was planned and carried out in sound mind.

My father's age played no part in the trial—he did not act out of befuddlement or in a state of senility—but it was, I think, taken into account at his sentencing. The court wanted to offer him the prospect of spending his last days with his family, a free man. His sentence may be reduced after a year or two, and we cling to the words 'day release'. My father would spend his days with us and in the evening I would drive him back to Tegel. 'To Tegel' is another phrase we're fond of using. Others say it and mean the airport. We mean the prison.

I must confess that I am not innocent of this manslaughter. I could have prevented what happened, but I didn't want to. When my father came to see us in late September last year, I knew what he was intending to do. It was a sunny day, and our windows were open, letting in all the noise of the street. The roads in our part of Berlin are cobbled, and the rumbling of the traffic is sometimes a torture to me when I work at home. My wife thinks I'm oversensitive. I once told her that Schopenhauer regarded sensitivity to noise as a sign of intelligence: the more sensitive a person was, the more intelligent he was likely to be. 'Are you trying to tell me—' she began. 'No,' I replied, 'I'm not.' Before long it had developed into one of those exchanges that can make married life so unpleasant. I later apologised. It wasn't a nice thing to say, but perhaps it was true.

I was expecting my father. He had let me know he was coming the day before, and soon after he'd left home my mother rang to tell me he'd be with me in two hours at the latest. This was a recent habit. My mother didn't think my father should be driving anymore, and if he didn't turn up at the expected time I was to initiate search-and-rescue operations immediately. Rebecca and I agreed with my mother and didn't like letting the children in the car with him, but my father knew nothing of this. It would have hurt and upset him—he still saw himself as a first-rate driver.

While I was waiting for my father, I wondered whether a man who no longer drove well could be a good marksman. Not that it was likely to be a tricky shot. He'd manage. I also caught myself picturing the drive going wrong in some way so that he wouldn't have to prove himself as a marksman at all. It would only take a minor accident to prevent his arrival and foil the murder plot. I always thought of the anticipated act as murder back then—it was only afterwards that our lawyer pointed out to me that it might technically be considered manslaughter, and that manslaughter was less severely punished.

But I wasn't really hoping for an accident. I wanted this murder. I'd been thinking about it for long enough, and now it had to happen. My wife had taken the children to stay with her mother—the circumstances couldn't have been better.

My father's drive, his last for the time being, would ideally be a smooth one. I'd followed the radio bulletins, and there were no traffic jams.

A few cars rumbled past and eventually I saw my father park his Ford outside our house. It's a lovely late nineteenth-century house: wooden beams, red walls, a turret, bay windows, dormers. We live on the upper ground floor in a spacious flat with rather imposing high ceilings, stucco mouldings and private access to the garden. Above our flat is a second storey, and there are flats in the attic and basement too—four households in all.

When I opened the door and saw my father standing there, I wondered where he had put his gun. He usually wore it in a holster under his left arm, but it might also have been in his overnight bag. In the past he had often carried a little leather pouch with him, such as pipe smokers like to use for a small assortment of pipes and tampers and tobacco, but in his there was a Walther PPK—or a Glock or a Colt. We had given him the pouch one Christmas, my mother, my sister, my little brother and I, though I've forgotten the precise year. He had used it for a while, presumably to make us feel our present was appreciated, but he soon went back to using his holster. From his point of view, it made more sense to carry the gun under his arm where he could get at it more quickly. The pouch needed unzipping, wasting precious seconds that could have cost him his life. I assume that was his logic.

My father was wearing a checked jacket, grey cloth trousers and comfortable shoes of the kind that provide a firm and secure footing. I think he wanted to look respectable when he was arrested—not like a thug who had stumbled into a crime, but like a mature man who had thought through what he had done. A man who had, what is more, done the right thing, even if others might not see it that way.

When we said hello we were, as so often, uncertain whether to shake hands or hug. My father held out his right hand, hesitantly, and I was about to take it but changed my mind, and at the same time my father changed his mind too, and we withdrew our hands and hugged each other in an almost disembodied embrace, without squeezing, without touching cheeks, looking hastily away when it was over. That was all we were capable of at the time. He came in and I made him an espresso while he unpacked homemade jam from his bag—cherry and quince. I wondered at the way my mother had taken even this opportunity to send us jars of the jam she produced so tirelessly, but that's my mother for you. We sat at the kitchen table and I told him the latest about the children. That was a safe topic between us—we didn't have many. In the evening we watched a football match: Bayern versus Bremen. We drank half a bottle of red wine and then went to bed. Neither of us mentioned Dieter Tiberius.

The next day my father sat on the sofa reading *Auto Motor and Sport*. As always when he came to visit, he had brought a pile of magazines with him. He could make them last all day; I think he reads every article. Before I go to see him now, I buy up half a newsagent's, mainly magazines about cars and guns, but also political magazines. My father is very interested in politics. Maybe they're not such unhappy hours for him, sitting in his cell reading, with no one to disturb him and no need to feel guilty about frittering away time that others would have liked to spend with him—his wife, for example, and, once upon a time, his children.

That day, the second day of his visit, nothing happened. Dieter Tiberius was lying low in the basement. I couldn't hear him moving around, but his toilet was flushed now and again, so he must have been in. In fact, he was always in. Over supper that night my father told me about developments in cylinder-head technology, or maybe it was carburettor technology—I can't remember—and then about new Israeli settlements on the West Bank. That took him far back into the history of the Middle East; my father likes reading history books. We drank the rest of the red wine, and then, when it was nearly midnight and my father had said all he had to say on the subject of the Israeli–Palestinian conflict, we went to bed. I was surprised. What was he waiting for? We hadn't talked anything over, but it was perfectly clear why he was here. Our family had come to a tacit understanding. Surely I couldn't be mistaken?

The next morning I got up early and went out in the

garden. It hadn't rained for a few days and I put the sprinkler on, making water rain down on the grass, flowerbeds and shrubs. I think I was hoping to hear a shot, so that it would be over at last, but I heard only the birds and the occasional rumbling of a car on the cobblestones. I walked round the outside of the house, passing the basement windows. There are four altogether: on the left, Dieter Tiberius had his bedroom, in the middle was the kitchen, and on the right, the living room, which had two windows, one at the front of the house and one at the side. The windows are small and low, just above the ground. Dieter Tiberius lived in gloom. I didn't see him on my way round; I would have had to stoop, which I didn't, of course. Maybe he saw my feet; I don't know. At that point he had about ten minutes to live.

When I got back to our flat, my father was sitting at the kitchen table. In front of him lay a pistol—a Walther PPK, calibre 7.65 mm Browning, but I only learnt that later, from the indictment. The prosecutor was keen to demonstrate his own knowledge of firearms—knowledge that, despite having the father I had, I didn't possess. I knew nothing about pistols and had no desire to.

I asked my father whether he wanted an espresso, and he did. I had switched on the machine, a beautiful Domita from Italy, soon after getting out of bed, to give it time to warm up. I unscrewed the filter holder and swapped the small filter for the big one, because I wanted an espresso too. Then I pushed the filter holder against the mill, setting it grinding and roaring. The ground coffee trickled into the filter until it was full to the brim. I took the tamper—heavy-duty metal with a rosewood handle—and pressed the coffee firm. I screwed the filter holder into the machine, placed two cups under the spouts and pressed the start button. The machine growled and the coffee ran brown and oily into the cups—always a glorious sight. You and your espresso fetish, my wife says, sometimes mockingly. People like me have to make a fetish out of everything, which doesn't just get on other people's nerves—it gets on mine too. We sipped our coffee in silence, the pistol on the table like a metal question mark. Should we really?

What happened next is best related in the words of the indictment: At about 8.40 am, the accused, Hermann Tiefenthaler (my father, that is), left the flat of his son, Randolph Tiefenthaler, with the Walther PPK, then in his lawful possession, and descended to the basement, where he induced the tenant, Dieter Tiberius, to open the door to his flat, either by knocking or ringing the bell, and then killed Tiberius with a close-range shot to the head. Tiberius died instantly.

I rang the police. My father had asked me to, but it was in any case clear that this was the line we would take: no crazy getaway, no cover-up. We stood by the act. We still do—I can say that without reservation.

The policeman who picked up the phone, Sergeant Leidinger, greeted me almost affably. He knew me well, and he knew the house—he'd been here a lot over the past few months and sometimes found our case cause for amusement, but he immediately grew serious when he heard that I had a death to report. I used those exact words, quite deliberately: 'I have a death to report.'

'Your wife?' Sergeant Leidinger asked, and I could hear his alarm, which gave me, I must admit, a certain satisfaction, after all the doubts the authorities had about the gravity of our situation.

'No,' I said, 'not my wife, thank goodness—it's Dieter Tiberius.'

For a few seconds there was silence, and I'd love to know what Leidinger was thinking then.

'We'll be right with you,' he said.

My father packed his bag and put on his checked jacket. Then he sat down at the kitchen table again, the Walther PPK in front of him. I made him another espresso. We had sometimes sat there like that in the past, before he set off for home—usually with my mother, because he never came without her—and funnily enough, I now said some of the things I always said: 'Have you got everything? Sure you haven't forgotten anything?'

My father went to have a last look in the bathroom and found his shaving foam.

'You can't check too often,' I said.

'Who knows when I'd have got any,' he said.

It had just occurred to me that you might not be allowed a wet shave in prison because of the razor blades—I knew nothing about life in prison—when the doorbell rang. Sergeant Leidinger and his colleague Rippschaft, who was also well known to me, were the first to arrive. Later, others came: policemen in uniform, plain-clothes detectives, a doctor, forensic investigators, pathologists.

My father told Sergeant Leidinger that he had shot the basement tenant. He said nothing else and was quiet throughout the proceedings. They didn't put handcuffs on him, perhaps because of his age, and for that I was thankful. We hugged when he left, properly this time. It was a long, loving embrace, the first of our life. We clung to one another and he said something that may sound strange to outsiders. 'I'm so proud of you,' he said—a statement that can only be understood as a kind of closing summary, a father's attempt to take stock of his relationship with his son before disappearing into prison. He had never said it before—or, indeed, anything like it. Maybe he wanted to make clear to me that, up until the appearance of Dieter Tiberius, he had considered my life a success, an absolute success, and that Dieter Tiberius was a mere episode in that life and no more—an episode which, thanks to a well-placed shot, was now over. He wanted to make clear to me that, in spite of the long silence between us, he was aware of that success—and he wanted to encourage me to continue along the path I had taken. I think that's why he said what he did.

3

ARE THERE TEARS IN MY EYES? I don't think so. It felt like it for a moment, as I was writing those last sentences, but I was mistaken. A little moisture, perhaps, a film over the eyes—normal, entirely normal. I am sitting at my desk in my study. It is just past eleven in the evening and the children have, of course, been in bed for quite some time. Rebecca came in a few minutes ago and said goodnight, kissing me, her hand on my cheek. 'Enjoy your writing,' she said, standing in the doorway looking back—rather a trite remark for her.

Perhaps she is a little uneasy because she doesn't know exactly why I'm writing this account or what will be in it.

All I've told her is that I need to get this off my chest. 'This' for us is the Tiberius case. I was telling my wife the truth when I said that, but maybe not the whole truth. I didn't mention that all has not yet been said—that something is missing. We have, of course, talked about it a lot, an awful lot, and we have heaped our grief and anger and fears on one another. Our marriage, which also had a rough ride, could and did stand the test. Still, there are some things I can't bring myself to say out loud.

I was never a great talker. It would not be wrong to maintain the opposite—at any rate, I wouldn't blame anyone who did. I listen for a long time before I speak, and talking in front of large groups doesn't come easy to me, but I can do it. It's not as bad as all that. I'm not uncommunicative. All I'm saying is that I'm not one for chatting, not the kind whose words roll off his tongue. Talking doesn't come as a matter of course to me, like walking—it is an effort, but an effort I accept without too much difficulty and sometimes even with pleasure. Perhaps that's why I'm writing this. Or perhaps it has something to do with the fact that Rebecca is still missing a few details from me.

It is nice, sitting here. It is quiet in our street now, nothing rumbling over the cobblestones. My neighbours' cars— massive cars, gargantuan, some of them—are parked at the kerb like the little brothers and sisters of the houses. Why have cars grown so large in recent years? Why are they as tall as men or as long as trucks, or both? When will people leave their houses because these four-wheel drives make such wonderful places to live? These are the dejected thoughts of a man whose livelihood depends on the building of houses. I am an architect. Perhaps they are also drunken thoughts, although I have resolved never to drink more than half a bottle of the glorious Black Print when I'm working on this report. One small glass is all I've had this evening, but a wine that is 14.5 per cent alcohol is not to be sneezed at.

Nonsense, I'm not drunk. I look out of the window at the street lamp, a gas lamp—a straight green pole, not overly ornate; a glass top; a little metal roof; warm, mellow light. There is a proposal to take these street lamps away from us, because gaslight is, apparently, more detrimental to the environment than electric light. Perhaps it is. But we fight the proposal. We haven't founded a civic action group—we're not that given to drama on this street—but the man opposite, a radiologist, collected signatures, and of course I signed. The way I see it, the point of the street lamps is not only to provide light, but also to give warmth. That, if I am not mistaken, is how it has always been, ever since people first sat around a fire. Light should make us feel cosy, not chilly. But electric light, especially from the new light bulbs, makes you shudder with cold.

Now I hear a ticking sound—it's the claws of our dog on the parquet. He's jumped down from one of the children's beds and is going into the kitchen to have a drink—our Benno, a Rhodesian ridgeback, a big, strong dog. He isn't trained to attack, but he has made us feel safe again. Even after the death of our downstairs neighbour, we remained a nervous family. Now we aren't. We wouldn't have Benno, if it hadn't been for Dieter Tiberius.

I am, then, writing this account because I hope writing will come easier to me than talking. But before I can fill in the missing details for my wife, I must get the backstory out of the way. A crime was committed, a crime we wanted, and, as with every crime, there was a chain of events leading up to it. I want to tell the whole story, not just the missing part, so that the missing part can be understood, put in perspective. It is good to sit here writing, looking out at the gas lamp, at the warm light it casts over the large cars parked outside my neighbours' houses. The street looks so serene at night, in the glow of the lamp. From the radiologist's living room comes the flickering grey light of a television.

I too am fond of reading history books, like my father, and I am, of course, familiar with the simplest trap a historian can fall into. You look back at a major event—a world war, for example—and everything that happened before it seems to bear its imprint. You are almost certain to come across a great many events leading up to that war that make it appear inevitable. I, Randolph Tiefenthaler, forty-five years old, architect, married man, father of two, and determined to become the historian of my own life, do not want to fall into that trap. On the other hand, a major event does not come out of nowhere—it has to have causes. It has to have a history, and that history often begins decades before. It is always both, I think: chance and inevitability. If we had seen Dieter Tiberius before buying the flat, we wouldn't have bought it—no doubt about it. That we didn't see him was chance. That he ended up having to die has something to do with my own history, I suppose. I can't deny that.

4

I HARDLY DARE WRITE THIS, because it sounds so terribly banal, but my life began with the fear of a war, with the fear of weapons. In October 1962, while my mother was heavily pregnant with me, my father bought several boxes of tinned food and crates of bottled water and stacked them in the cellar, because they wanted to be prepared for a nuclear war. The Cuban missile crisis had just begun, and my parents had the naive, almost touching hope that they would be able to survive a nuclear attack in their cellar. They planned to wait there a few days until the fires had gone out and the radioactivity had subsided, and then live on in a ravaged world with their daughter—my sister, who was a year old at the time—and their son, who would have been born in that cellar.

It was the cellar of a Berlin tower block, a dingy hole behind a gate of wooden bars, where my parents kept their bikes and the things they didn't have room for in their flat, but which were too precious to part with, not so much from a material point of view as a sentimental one. Among these things was a basic encyclopaedia, whose most recent volume arrived in the post every month. This encyclopaedia stood out less for its dependable knowledge than for its lavish binding, which supposedly warranted the high price. My grandma had let someone at the door talk her into a subscription, and had given it to her daughter-in-law, but my mother, in spite of her mere nine years' schooling, was not taken in by the encyclopaedia's handsome livery, and stacked it in the cellar, where it could be dug out for consultation should it ever be needed. Potatoes were also stored in this cellar, I believe. But it was not to be the place where I made my way into the world—that was a hospital. When I left my mother's womb on 30 October, the crisis was over. Khrushchev had announced two days before that he would withdraw his missiles from Cuba. Kennedy's persistence had paid off.

Did these events seal my fate? Was I a child destined to

live a life of fear? No, my parents saw things differently. For them, I was a peace baby, a symbol of hope. Khrushchev had backed down so that I might live a happy, peaceful life, my mother said, when she told me about those times—jokingly, of course, as mothers will say such things jokingly. The idea that Khrushchev had, in some deeper sense, withdrawn for her benefit and that of her family did not seem abstruse to my mother.

It is chance that I was in my mother's womb at the time of the Cuban missile crisis, when the entire world was preoccupied with its imminent destruction. The question is whether that fact isn't of crucial relevance to my life all the same. There is no doubt that my mother was frightened as the crisis ran its course—she was living in Berlin, the city on the front line of the Cold War. If the Russians didn't destroy Berlin to spare East Germany, then the Americans would do it to eliminate East Germany. It made no difference whether the missiles came from the east or the west—my parents were expecting to end up as war victims.

A pregnant woman is afraid twice over, I suppose— afraid for herself and afraid for her child, whom she wants to protect, but cannot protect well. She is particularly vulnerable because she is particularly immobile. That was my mother's situation when I was living in her womb. I don't know what effect a mother's fears have on her foetus—I haven't read anything on the subject—but one suspects they cannot be entirely without consequence. To be honest, I'd never thought about it until recently. It is only since meeting Dieter Tiberius, only since toying with the idea of my life as a war story, that I have begun to grapple with such things. Were we too scared of him? And where did our fear come from? Was my own fear born of my mother's fear, all those years ago? But come on—that would make all babies born in the last months of 1962 babies of fear, and I'm sure that's not the case.

Even now, I insist that I had a normal childhood—a childhood without much money, with the odd scuffle, few problems at school, loving parents, a big sister, and before too long a little brother. We lived on a new estate in Berlin's north-west: red tower blocks interspersed with lawns, a playground and a stadium belonging to Wacker 04, the local football club, where I played in goal on the youth teams. My parents evidently didn't consider the town dangerous, although it was at the centre of the Cold War, because I remember getting the bus a lot without them, and that must have been before my tenth birthday. Soon after that birthday, we moved to the northern outskirts of the city, where my parents bought a semidetached house. That makes it easier to place memories, because I have a fairly clear idea of what was before the move and what came after.

The bus rides were definitely before. I have forgotten why I travelled about such a lot—I ought to ask my mother some time—but I certainly spent a great many hours on those

pale yellow double-decker buses. I would jostle to be first at
the bus stop as soon as the bus arrived, and then rush up the
narrow stairs to claim a front seat. A ride in any other seat
was a lost ride—I let buses drive past if I saw that both front
benches were taken. Those benches had the best view and
only there did you sometimes get that slight tingling in your
belly from the feeling that you were sitting at the edge of a
moving precipice. It was glorious.

I remember the smell of chlorine on the way back from the
public swimming pool, burning my fingers on bags of chips,
and eating my first hamburger at the German–American
festival (long before McDonald's arrived). I remember the
quiet of the local library and the guilt I felt when a book I'd
borrowed was overdue.

I remember, too, rides on the underground, especially the
empty stations in East Berlin that our trains passed through
without stopping. In the dark of those stations I saw sandbags
and soldiers with rifles, and that must have been my first
waking nightmare—that my train would be stranded there
and all the passengers made to get out and left at the mercy
of this world of darkness. That's all East Germany was to me
at the time: the dark of their underground stations and the
great emptiness around the Brandenburg Gate.

My parents took us to the gate, my brother and sister and
me, and we all climbed onto the viewing platform and peered
over the Wall. No one there. The square was empty, the streets

beyond too. It made no sense to me when I was a child. Why did the East Germans build an enormous wall, put up watchtowers, pile up sandbags and have soldiers patrol when they had nothing to protect except deserted stations and empty squares and streets? There was something bad about the world behind this wall—that much I had gleaned from remarks dropped by my parents. But what? I didn't know and in fact I didn't care. When I wasn't passing through one of those empty stations, I forgot that I lived behind a wall and that this wall was, as my parents had told me, a symbol of hostility.

Only once did I experience that hostility at first hand. It was probably in 1969 or 1970, when I was about eight years old, before the transit agreement signed a few years later that made it easier for us to travel through East Germany. We were going to visit my grandparents—not my father's parents, but my mother's, who lived in Wuppertal. I had been to visit them once before, but that time we had flown. As my parents packed our Ford 12M, I noticed how nervous they were, especially my father, who always got cross when he was nervous. He snarled at me and dragged my sister off the back seat because she'd got in too early, before my mother had stowed the last bags and parcels in the back foot wells. My father fetched and carried, my mother stowed things; that was the arrangement. He had strength and she had skill—and the optimism needed to continue packing a car that was clearly chock full.

My father was in a sweat—not from the fetching and carrying, which was over, but from watching. The 12M's springs and shock absorbers were sagging, and there were still bags in the parking area outside our house. I remember that car park as largely empty, but some wise person had designed it for a great automotive future—a future which did indeed come. There are hardly any free parking spaces in Berlin these days, not even in our little street, which isn't exactly densely populated. Eventually my father walked away, because he couldn't bear to watch my mother stowing things anymore. That wasn't unusual—my father often walked away when things got difficult, but he always came back. We knew he would, so we weren't worried.

My mother went to fetch him after cramming the last thing—her vanity case—into the Ford. My sister, my four-year-old brother and I stood by the 12M and watched our parents negotiating with one another on the far side of the big, empty car park. My sister fiddled with her plaits, my little brother sucked his thumb and I plunged my hands into my pockets. We couldn't hear what our parents were talking about, but we knew how it would end. My mother took my father in her arms and held him for a while, and then they came back hand in hand.

My father was still nervous, though. I noticed this as we drove down the motorway. When we were waiting in the queue at the checkpoint on the East German border, he broke into a sweat again. A face appeared at the side window beneath a big military cap. We were to get out, said the man in the military cap. When we had got out, he said we were to take our things out of the car.

'Everything?' my mother asked, because in situations like this my father wouldn't or couldn't talk.

'Everything,' said the man.

'All right then, everything,' said my mother.

I was afraid now. I was afraid of this man who was giving us orders so curtly. I was afraid, too, that my father would pull out his gun and start a shootout. He couldn't win, that much was clear to me, because there were a lot of men in military caps standing about. They carried pistols—I had already noticed that—and some of them even had rifles or machine guns. I didn't know at the time that my father, who always wore a pistol in a holster, did not have it on him that day, because nobody would be so mad as to approach an East German border post with a pistol holstered under their arm—certainly not with his wife in the passenger seat and three children in the back of the car. So my fear was unwarranted. My father couldn't start a shootout—he had no gun to hand. It was only years later that I found out from my mother that there had, in fact, been every reason to be afraid. My father, who couldn't bear the thought of spending several days unarmed, had stayed at work after hours in the dealership's garage and welded himself a secret compartment in the 12M. In this compartment he had put a revolver, which goes a long way towards explaining his nervousness.

Mind you, the people unpacking and repacking their cars in front of us and behind us were also nervous. It was a dreadful situation. We children looked on as our capable mother serenely undid her great feat of packing, while our father was paralysed with fear or anger or both and could only do as she asked, on autopilot, even though unloading a car is so much easier than loading it. Then my parents were instructed (again, curtly) that they were to unpack the suitcases. My mother set to work, on her own, while my father sat on the edge of the passenger seat, his feet on the asphalt, head in his hands. Beneath the gaze of two men in military caps, my mother took trousers, shirts and skirts out of our suitcases, using only her left hand because her right arm was around my little brother, who had begun to cry.

Sometimes, by no means rarely, we host soirees in our flat. They are really just big dinner parties, but we have always called them soirees, using the rather pompous name ironically, to begin with, and then for tradition's sake. On one such occasion, the conversation turned to the subject of dignity, and I talked about my mother. I described how she had squatted there in front of our suitcases, pulling out one item of clothing after another, briefly presenting them to the border guards and then laying them on a pile beside the suitcase. She did this with everything, even her underwear. Garment after garment she pulled out, unmoved and imperturbable, holding each one up to the border guards and then setting it aside. Her youngest child was snivelling at her side; her husband was in a state of depressed shock; her daughter desperately needed the toilet but didn't dare ask if she could go; and her elder son was terrified that under the next bra, under the next shirt, a weapon might appear. When my mother had shown the border guards the entire contents of our luggage, she packed the suitcases, bags and parcels again and stowed everything once more in our Ford, with the same skill and optimism as before, looking for all the world as if she were enjoying herself. My father didn't watch her— he was already at the wheel, staring straight ahead, past the checkpoint. After my mother had stowed everything, she said a polite goodbye, wished the guards a nice day and got in the car. We drove off at a hundred kilometres an hour, not one kilometre over the limit.

At this point in my story, one of our guests, the director of a film production company, interrupted me and said: 'The West Germans slunk through East Germany for decades on terrified best behaviour, doing as they were told for fear that they'd be fined, and now they reproach the East Germans who did exactly the same for fear they'd be arrested and locked up in Bautzen.'

'Are you from the east?' asked another guest, a doctor.

'No,' said the director.

'But I am,' said a journalist who presented a late-night cultural show on the radio, 'and I agree with you. The West Germans were like East Germans the moment they set foot across the border. Given half the chance, we Germans like to subjugate ourselves.'

During the heated discussion that ensued, I sat feeling rather annoyed. I had told our border-crossing story to show how wonderfully composed my mother had been—that she should be accused of willing subjugation hadn't occurred to me. Eventually the journalist said it was possible to display dignity in submitting to authority, as my mother had done. Everyone agreed and I felt a little better about our evening.

I still remember the ghastly drive from the checkpoint to my grandparents' house, more than five hours away. My sister still desperately needed the toilet, but my father refused to pull into an East German road stop. I am afraid she soiled her pants. But what I remember most from the time with my grandparents and our subsequent seaside holiday in the Netherlands is my aunt—my mother's sister—saying at a big family gathering: 'Randolph never has anything to say.' They are words I have heard many times since—from my wife, among others.

5

MY FONDEST CHILDHOOD MEMORIES—and by childhood
I mean our time living in the flat on the estate—are of my
visits to the Ford dealership where my father worked. He
started out as a mechanic there, but I only ever knew him
as a car salesman and, to quote the words he said to me not
so long ago, I was proud of him. I would get the bus there
by myself, and I enjoyed going, because I liked the new cars,
their shininess, the smell of metal and leather and rubber, the
hint of animal about them, their dumb inertia which could,

I imagined, give way without a moment's notice to a wild chase.

My father was in charge of these huge predatory beasts, although he was not, as I was well aware, in charge of the business. That was my father's boss, a man named Mr Marschewski, the son of the owner. But it was my father who was in charge of the car yard—the animals, the other salesmen, the customers. I liked watching him pace slowly from one car to the next—17M or 15M to begin with, later Consul, Capri and Granada, and later still Scorpio and Mondeo, but by then I had stopped being proud of him. My father knew all about those cars—about every new Ford on the market. Back then, in the sixties, people were willing to marvel when someone explained an automobile to them—because it was their first, or because they had not yet lost their awe of industrial technology. My father was not a salesman for me: he was a man who could make others marvel, something like a magician, perhaps.

I am afraid to say he was also the man who took me along to the firing range at the rod and gun club every Saturday. I had already managed to prevent him making a hunter out of me. Aged six, I had sat in a raised hide with him, waiting for a deer, and done nothing but cry, so that he had ended up taking me home. But if I was spared being a hunter, I was to be a sports marksman. Every Saturday, we drove down the motorway, took the Wannsee exit and followed the rail embankment south. On the back seat lay a leather case secured with a padlock.

I don't remember much about the firing range and I wouldn't dream of driving there to refresh my memories. If I make an effort, I see a wooden shack where you could buy sausages, and there were two or three shooting ranges as well as a field where archers practised. The first hour was tolerable. My father shot and I hung around the archers, watching them or helping them gather up the arrows that had missed their target. It was quiet there, which made it all right. The horror began when my father fetched me from the field and we went to the shooting range.

As I was still too weak to hold a pistol, a sandbag was placed on the shelf in front of me. I was eight or nine—tall, but slight. I put on ear protectors, and my father loaded the pistol, almost tenderly, and gave it to me. I always felt panicked as I took it in my hands, knowing I could injure or kill someone—including myself. In spite of the ear protectors, I would hear the shot clearly—painfully clearly, even. The recoil would jerk my arms back, and that hurt too. My father would correct my posture before I took a shot. After I had fired, he would upbraid me for getting everything wrong as usual, and before long he would be exasperated: he was not a patient teacher. I could hardly hear him, because of the ear protectors, but I didn't want to take them off because there was constant shooting to the right and left of me, so I understood next to nothing of what he said. I saw only his face, saw it change as his gathering impatience eventually tipped over into anger.

On a bad day, he would walk away—if I still hadn't been breathing properly even after the third or fourth shot—*breathe in, breathe out, breathe halfway in, hold your breath*—or if I had hunched my back at the last second in a defensive gesture. Then I stood there alone, helpless, surrounded by silent, unmoving men in shooting glasses, their focus narrow and intense, with neither eyes nor heart for my plight. Maybe these men were practising to be murderers, I thought. My father would, of course, come back—he always came back—but that didn't make it any better here at the shooting range. He'd calm down, to a certain point, but then it would begin all over again: the unintelligible words, the look on his face, the way it contorted as his impatience inevitably morphed into anger—or rather, wrath, for anger is human, whereas wrath is something that seizes the gods, and that is how my father seemed to me in his omnipotence—a wrathful god, an Ares. There was no way out: I had to shoot, so I shot. Sometimes I even hit the target.

After this ordeal, we sat in the wooden shack. I ate a sausage and drank lemonade, while my father drank a beer—only ever one—and cleaned the pistols we had used. There were other men sitting in the shack, but we usually sat on our own. My father wasn't—and still isn't—a sociable man. He went to the shooting range to shoot, not to meet people.

There was sometimes a woman in the shack, too, whose presence always disconcerted me. In the books and comics I read, women didn't shoot—and if they did put in an appearance, there was kissing soon afterwards, something I found embarrassing, and also irksome, because it held up the plot, which was what interested me. The pursuit of criminals or Indians was interrupted until the hero had finally done with all that awful kissing. And so the woman at the firing range was suspicious to me. Why did she come to our table and knock on the wooden tabletop? What did she want from my father? He knocked too, and then the woman went on her way and knocked on the tables where other men were sitting. In the end she sat down on the corner bench, behind the round table, where there was always the most talking and laughter. I kept an eye on her.

As my father cleaned his pistols and drank his beer, he made plans about the gun he would soon buy me—a birthday and Christmas present combined, because guns are expensive. It would be my first gun, a pistol of my own. I have forgotten the names of the models he pondered in a tender voice—all I remember is the atmosphere at our table. I had put the weekly torment behind me, and I felt the warmth of my father's love and approval as I discussed with him the pros and cons of various small arms for a nine-year-old.

Even if I didn't want a pistol, not under any circumstances, I liked it when my father indulged in flights of fancy. He could imagine wonderful things and get as enthusiastic about them as if they were already real. Despite my disappointing performance on the range less than an hour ago—and repeated every week—he envisaged me winning the German youth championship with my pistol some day, and it made him happy. I saw myself with a trophy in my hands.

My favourite times with my father, my favourite times all round, were our Sunday walks in the woods. We would all set off together, but after half an hour my father would stride ahead and I was the only one who could keep up, while my sister and little brother trotted along behind at my mother's side. Once it was just the two of us, out in front, my father would dream up journeys for us to go on together. These were, without exception, journeys of adventure. My father had read a lot of adventure books as a boy and they had made an adventurer of him. If he happened to be an adventurer who had not yet had an adventure, it was, I knew, for a good reason: he lacked a travelling companion. But soon that would change. I was nine years old, and next year I would be ten. Ten was already pretty old—old enough for first adventures. As I walked along beside my father, listening to his stories of our future journeys, I was preparing myself for the role of his travelling companion.

Those journeys took us into the mountains, high up

into the snow and the merciless cold, where you could only survive in special sleeping bags and tents; they took us into the wilderness where we didn't see a soul for days on end, only buffalo (sometimes we shot one—we were good marksmen—and barbecued buffalo loin over our camp fire in the evening); they took us into whitewater canyons, where we skilfully steered our canoe through the rapids. I listened breathlessly. It was better than the tales I borrowed from the library and read again and again until they were overdue. My father's stories made me think that I, too, could live a life of adventure—or something approaching it.

6

I HAD A HAPPY CHILDHOOD, really I did—the only problem was the target practice. My mother sometimes clobbered me with wooden coathangers, but in those days that was the usual punishment meted out to a boy who behaved badly at school and had no qualms about signing his mother's name beneath the red F at the bottom of a school essay: *Read and acknowledged, Elisabeth Tiefenthaler, 14 April 1972.* I was good at forging, but occasionally I was caught all the same and it was then that the coathangers came into action.

My father never hit me, by the way—only my mother. I didn't consider it abuse. All my friends were given regular hidings; that's just the way it was. It wasn't until I was seventeen or eighteen and fighting major battles with my mother that I resented the beatings and reproached her for them. It was a way of manoeuvring my mother, who had come to regret the beatings, into an awkward position—a way of turning my childhood pains to my advantage. My moral stance was more tactical ploy than deeply held conviction, and nothing to be proud of. Though I myself have never hit my children, sometimes I have come pretty close.

I think it was in September 1972 that I told my father one Saturday morning that I wouldn't be accompanying him to the firing range. Until then I hadn't dared, but my tenth birthday was approaching and I had to reckon on being given a pistol at Christmas at the latest. After that there would be practically no getting out of our weekly target practice. 'What do you think a pistol like that costs?' my father would have been able to say, and for a child who has grown up in financial straits that is a weighty argument.

For a long time I thought money was tight because of the meagre wages earned by a car salesman, even one who was a magician. And it's true, car salesmen don't get rich. The basic wage is low, but with the commission on sales it's possible to make a decent living. Our problem was that my father was constantly buying new guns—pistols, revolvers, hunting shotguns. He never told us how many guns he had. Not even my mother knew precisely. Later, in the eighties, she guessed that it was at least thirty.

Because we had so little money, we couldn't go on holiday every year. I remember riding my bike all around the neighbourhood in the holidays, desperately looking for another boy like me who hadn't been able to go away. This is one of the very few things I hold against my father. He should have taken us to the seaside more often—to Amrum, on the North Sea, where I once went on a school trip and slid down the big white dunes, or to Noordwijk, the Dutch seaside resort we had visited with my mother's family. Ten or fifteen guns should have been enough—even for a man like him, who not only liked guns but needed them.

But he did appreciate—and this speaks in his favour— that his elder son did not want to be a marksman. He asked me why I didn't want to accompany him to the firing range, and I said, at once defiant and timid: 'It's no fun.' My father looked at me, not cross but disappointed, and then he drove to the firing range on his own. I never went back and my father never asked me to accompany him again. He didn't punish me, though, as I'd feared—didn't give me the cold shoulder, or stop telling me stories as we hiked through the woods. Those glorious tales of our future adventures continued, and I remained his companion. That, at least, was my impression.

It was only years later, through my son, that I discovered

how disappointed my father had been when I gave up our weekend trips to the shooting range. When Paul was five, my father gave him a target, a cardboard square of maybe fifteen centimetres by fifteen centimetres, yellowish around the edge with a black circle in the centre divided by thin white lines. There were six small holes in the cardboard, all within the black circle, all close to the centre, some of them touching each other. 'Grandad says you were good at shooting,' said Paul, when he showed me the target. I took it, quickly gave it back to him, turned and left the room. My father had kept that target for thirty-five years.

I can't remember being a good marksman. I remember my fear. I remember my father's wrath. That's memory for you.

It wasn't until some weeks after giving up target practice that I realised my sister was not around on Saturday mornings. I asked my mother and she told me she'd gone to the firing range with Dad. That seemed strange to me—she was a girl, wasn't she? But I didn't let it bother me. Perhaps she could learn to shoot. A girl couldn't become a travelling companion, though—that much was clear.

It's not worth saying much more about my childhood. Friends came and went, girls were first scorned and later loved—shy kisses, short letters. There were wooden coathanger days, and days when my mother played with us for hours on end: Chinese chequers, ludo, pick-up sticks. My father sat on the sofa and read. My memories are no more than vague fragments: onion-patterned orange wallpaper, green curtains, a husky voice from the radio saying that a man was being buried, an important man—Adenauer, I suppose, the first postwar chancellor, but I'm not sure— and my father freaking out, enraged, because students were fighting the police in the streets. That must have been in 1967 or '68. Willy Brandt was elected not too much later—I remember hearing his name often, and the footballer Franz Beckenbauer's. We didn't have television, so I watched the sports round-up at a friend's house, and *Star Trek*, too. My mother sewed us symbols like the ones Captain Kirk and Spock and the others wore on their chests: jagged yellow triangles that she cut out of cardboard and covered with cloth. I remember blue-uniformed air hostesses when we flew Pan Am to Hamburg on a school trip, and the memorial ceremony for the Israeli athletes killed by terrorists at the Olympic Games in Munich. I remember a few scuffles, which I lost (harmless), and being tested by a school psychologist (all well, was the report—but also a term I didn't understand until later: inhibited aggression). 'Not a problem,' the school psychologist told my mother. 'Not a problem,' she told me.

It was a normal childhood—I insist on that. My mother taught me to say my prayers, and every evening I thanked the good Lord for my happy life and prayed for it to carry on. That bears me out. There were times, later on, when I thought my childhood couldn't have been that happy, because my father and I were getting on so badly. I didn't want to admit that he had provided me with a happy childhood, but that was silly—and shabby of me, too. It was during my years in the peace movement, when I hated weapons, and the weekends we'd spent together on the firing range seemed to me like a form of child abuse.

But do you have the right to decide, looking back, that your childhood was unhappy, if you didn't feel unhappy at the time? I don't think you do. I really didn't like it at the firing range, but it was only a few Saturdays, and don't a lot of parents try to interest their children in their hobbies and pastimes? Why not shooting, which is, after all, an Olympic sport? And who's to say children don't suffer on tennis courts or ice rinks?

No, I won't let myself be talked out of the memory of a happy childhood—not that anyone apart from me has tried so far, with the exception of a therapist I went to see a few years back, when I was going through a troubled patch. He told me I should stop trying to see everything so positively. I only went back a few times.

7

WHEN WE BOUGHT THE FLAT, our children were two and five. We met the owners of the three other flats over coffee on the first floor, including the owner of the basement, a laundry manager in his late fifties, who looked as if he could afford more than a dingy little place underground. The others were elderly people who said there hadn't been children living there for ages and it was time there was life in the house again. They were nice, but nobody told us that the basement owner was not the basement tenant.

You might ask why an architect buys a flat rather than building a house, particularly since I specialise in family homes. I fear the truth is that I felt a certain uneasiness at the idea, as if I was afraid that someone like me might manage to botch his own house. But it was also a question of money. The kind of house I would like to build is out of my price range. I know only too well how sad it is when great ideas dwindle under the diktat of a meagre budget.

My clients often come to me with ideas for family homes that would cost a million euros, not even counting the land. They want three hundred square metres of living space, and mezzanines with beautiful vistas; they want the bottom quarter of the facade clad in slate, and a freestanding bathtub carved from precious wood in the ensuite bathroom. The tub alone costs nine thousand euros and is struck off the list in the first round of hard truths. The next round puts paid to the slate and the mezzanines, and so it goes on, until my clients settle for two hundred and twenty square metres over two storeys, which costs them four hundred and fifty thousand euros (not counting the land again) and leaves them fifty thousand euros over their budget. They manage, somehow—the bank coughs up, or Mum and Dad advance a share of their inheritance—and my clients end up moving into houses in the new classical style, perhaps with an expressive flourish here or there—a few rounded corners, for example. I prefer to spare myself such orgies of reduction.

I first saw Dieter Tiberius after we had been living in the new flat for six weeks. He had already met my wife several times. There was something strange about him, but he was friendly, she told me. What do you mean, *strange*? I asked. She shrugged, and I forgot about him. I didn't meet him myself until I got home from work one evening and inadvertently rang his doorbell. He climbed the stairs and opened the front door. No, that's not right—he flung it open.

'Shouldn't think you were wanting me,' he said.

I was flummoxed. I stared at him and said nothing. He was short and fat, but there was nothing flabby about his corpulence—he was tautly fat. He looked supple and elastic, like an ageing gymnast, and must have been about forty. He had a large head, a high forehead and hair that looked a bit like Elvis Presley's, because he wore it combed back. Something flashed in his eyes—something alien and repulsive. I can't say precisely what it was—cunning was part of it, that much is certain, and annoyance, maybe because I had disturbed him, but there was nothing unequivocally threatening in the way he looked at me, no brutality or malice. It was more like the will to survive, and fear, too—I don't know, exactly. Maybe that is just how I interpret it now, looking back. I only saw him a few times close up.

'I'm sorry,' I said eventually.

'That's all right,' he said with a grin.

I went up the stairs and knocked at our front door. I was

in shock—there's no other way of putting it. I immediately had the feeling that it had been a mistake to buy the flat, although Dieter Tiberius didn't look terrible or threatening— really he didn't. Maybe 'unusual' is the right word. Dieter Tiberius looked unusual. That is by no means a reason for not wanting to live upstairs from someone or for being afraid of him, but that's how it was with me.

We knew nothing about him. He clearly didn't go to work, and when he did leave the house, my wife told me, he returned shortly afterwards with bags from the supermarket— not from either of the two organic supermarkets in our neighbourhood, but from the discount store. The curtains of his flat were always drawn, but the glow from his television could be seen through them in the evenings, and sometimes we heard the sound too. The films he watched weren't bad— Hollywood classics rather than trash. He was keen on Dustin Hoffman—I often heard snatches of dialogue from *The Graduate, Marathon Man, Tootsie* or *Rain Man*.

In the first months, nothing happened, and I was reassured. He was pleasant to my wife—and to the children. Once he showed my son a short animal film on his computer; my wife didn't take issue with it, so I didn't either. He would bake biscuits and leave a plate outside our door with a note beneath it: *Here's to good neighbours.* We ate the plate clean. Dieter Tiberius could bake, no doubt about it. The children began to like him. When we had breakfast in the living room at the front of the flat on a Sunday, we always saw him leave the house at nine, and an hour and a half later he was back. We assumed that, unlike us, he went to church. We only go at Christmas, and indeed I saw him on Christmas Day, singing 'O, How Joyfully', like me. He was up in the gallery, looking over the balustrade at us down in the nave when I spotted him.

In January my wife told me that Dieter Tiberius had started baking more often for her and the children. When she got home, he would open the front gate with the buzzer in his flat.

'As if he were waiting for me,' said my wife.

There was often a tray of cake or pizza on our doormat when she came in. She felt watched.

'Shall I talk to him?' I asked.

She hesitated, thought about it and then said: 'No, he's only trying to be nice.'

Today I reproach myself for not intervening, not confronting him. It might have prevented things from getting out of hand, although probably not. All the same, I should have tried.

The first entry in my diary indicating that the situation had taken a dangerous turn is dated 11 February. At the back of the basement is a laundry room that belongs to us. For some time, Dieter Tiberius had been coming out of his flat when he heard my wife hanging up the washing in there. He would chat to her in a friendly, even cheerful way, and my wife did not, at first, find it awkward—she had company during a dull chore. On this particular day, however, when she took a pair of her underpants out of the washing machine and pulled them flat, Dieter Tiberius said: 'They must look good on you.' It was an impossible remark, an impertinence, revolting. My wife ignored it. She hung up the underpants, Dieter Tiberius changed the subject, and she carried on pegging out the rest of our clothes as if nothing had happened. In the evening my wife told me about it, and I should of course have stormed down to the basement and taken Dieter Tiberius to task, but I didn't. I had got home late, my wife was already in bed, and she didn't tell me until I was in bed too. I was horrified and said I would speak to him in the morning, but I didn't—my next mistake.

On 19 February my wife found a letter on the doormat, a love letter, which she showed me that evening. It was written in a neat, almost childlike hand. The spelling was accurate. Dieter Tiberius wrote that she was very beautiful and very nice and that he loved her, but he had grown up in a children's home and so was prone to excessive emotions. It was absurd—I had to laugh. A fat, ugly dwarf had fallen in love with my beautiful, intelligent wife. I expect I said as much to Rebecca. In the seven months that followed, we thought, said and did a great deal that contradicted the image we had of ourselves, and what I call our enlightened middle-class values. This was the moment it began—the cruel language and the arrogance were our first step towards barbarism.

I pondered the significance of his childhood in care. Did it make him more than usually dangerous, because he'd had it rough and knew how to survive, or less than usually dangerous, because he had no family to support him? I didn't—couldn't—come up with an answer, because I had no experience of people brought up in state care, but it reassured me a little that Dieter Tiberius was evidently conscious that he had overstepped the mark. I interpreted the reference to his background as an apology and, believing myself capable of handling such a man, took the letter down to the basement and knocked at his door. Nothing stirred. All was quiet in his flat. I couldn't hear the television. I rang the bell, called his name—nothing. I was sure he was in— he never went out in the evenings. So he was hiding, he was afraid. That, too, reassured me. I underestimated Dieter Tiberius from the beginning.

22 February: Found a book on our doormat for Rebecca, *The Great Gatsby* by F. Scott Fitzgerald. Puzzled over a possible message, but couldn't come up with anything. Sat up half the night reading the book, but found no connection.

10 March: Rebecca rang me at the office. I could tell she was upset. Tiberius had written her another letter. It says he was passing our door and happened to hear the words 'pull down your pants'. He thinks this might be a sign that we're abusing the children. He himself was sexually abused 'as a child in care' and is thus 'sensitised to such things, maybe over-sensitised'. I told her I'd come straight home and talk to him, in no uncertain terms. 'I've already done that,' she said. 'I screamed my head off at him.' Must have been hell for the poor bastard.

Today I am ashamed of these words. Back then I wrote them without thinking, because I knew only too well what it's like when my wife has a screaming fit.

I went home that day all the same. My secretary had called me a taxi and I rushed down to the street and waited impatiently. In the taxi I wondered whether to hit Dieter Tiberius, but I haven't hit anyone since I was ten, except in harmless fights with my little brother. I don't believe in resolving conflicts with violence, even though my time in the peace movement is long over. I'd shout at him, I thought in the taxi. But I've never shouted at anyone, not even my children. When things get difficult, I tend to be calm and cold—getting loud is not my thing. But maybe I could manage to raise my voice a bit, I thought, let him see that I'm angry. Maybe that would make an impression on him.

I regret to say that my initial fury at his obscene accusations had abated before I arrived home, and I had even begun to feel relieved. This ridiculous stunt somehow made him seem less of a threat.

I wrote in my diary later that he must be mad. I saw no danger, fearing only awkwardness and unease:

> Anyone who infers sexual abuse from 'pull down your pants' is a lunatic. They are words spoken a dozen times a day in a family with small children. No one seriously out to undermine us would come up with such a ludicrous accusation. But can we live under the same roof as a man who harbours such thoughts? Isn't it too revolting?

When I got home, I went straight up to our flat. I hugged my wife, and then my children, who knew nothing of what had happened and were surprised to see their father in the afternoon. My wife had calmed down. Dieter Tiberius had been up and apologised profusely. He didn't know how he could have come up with such nonsense either. He sometimes had 'episodes', presumably something to do with growing up in a home. All he wanted was to get on with his neighbours, and he would act accordingly in the future, most definitely.

'Should I talk to him anyway?' I asked my wife—another

mistake. I shouldn't have left the decision to her. She had given vent to her feelings by shouting at him, and felt reassured by their later conversation and his many apologies. She hoped he was chastened. I recklessly embraced this hope, rather than go downstairs.

In the five weeks that followed, nothing happened, and we considered ourselves vindicated. We had settled a disagreeable episode in a sensible way. Sometimes we heard snatches of dialogue from *Tootsie*, sometimes the toilet being flushed, but there were no more biscuits, no more books, no more letters for my wife, and Dieter Tiberius himself was no longer in evidence.

8

ON 15 APRIL OF THAT YEAR, I flew to Bali for a wedding, via Frankfurt and Singapore. I travelled alone, without my wife and children. After a brief discussion, we had agreed that a five-day trip with two fourteen-hour flights was too strenuous for small children, especially with the six hours' time difference. I must admit, however, that it suited me very well. We could certainly have managed with Paul and Fay, but it wasn't at all what I wanted, and, if I remember rightly, I was the one who first said we couldn't put our children through a journey like that. Rebecca went along with my view.

I ought, at this point, to say a few words about the state of our relationship at the time we got caught up in this maelstrom. Our marriage was, to put it cautiously, troubled, and I fear this was probably my fault. There was no breakdown as such, no constant bickering, no door-slamming, no running away, no hatred—none of that. It was simply that over the course of the years, I had withdrawn from the marriage. I don't mean from the children—I am a father who adores his children, plays with them, talks to them, is never happier than when he is with them. I mean the marriage itself—my relationship with my wife.

I don't know how it started. I don't think you ever know how things start, unless a bombshell is dropped and an affair exposed or something along those lines, but it wasn't like that with us. The best way of putting it is to say that I slunk out of my marriage by degrees, over a long period of time. I often tried to work out when I realised that something wasn't right—when it became clear to me that the answer to the question 'How are things at home?' had stopped corresponding with reality. The answer is invariably 'good' or 'great', with an optimistic smile to match. It was my answer too, well after it was no longer true.

A moment of minor revelation came one evening in Hedin, one of the city's top restaurants. It has a Michelin star and eighteen points in Gault Millau. The tables were filled with couples and groups in festive mood, because even if you don't arrive in festive mood, a dinner such as you get at Hedin makes you feel festive at once. Only one table was occupied by a solitary man, and he too was in festive mood, celebrating a private feast. He ate six courses: sea urchin with Sichuan pepper and pineapple, then abalone, then sea bass with Alba truffles and twenty-year-old rice wine, then partridge with Chinese honey and sprouts, then Kobe beef with beetroot and Périgord truffles and finally *caramel au beurre salé* with passionfruit and Japanese chestnuts—each course with its own wine selected by the sommelier. Between courses, the man sitting there alone drew in a soft lead pencil on a pad of paper. He was making sketches of a family house, dashing them off, and he looked satisfied, even happy. Although the chair opposite him clearly lacked an inhabitant, he lacked for nothing. I was that man.

I only felt gloomy once that evening, when it occurred to me that it was, perhaps, a little strange to be enjoying in solitary splendour the hours traditionally spent à deux, while my wife sat at home with a book, watching over our sleeping children. It was then I realised that I did not like being with my wife, that I was avoiding her, that my happiest hours were spent alone or with the children. I did not pursue the thought, deliberately suppressing it. I took the abalone shell home; it is patterned with black and mother-of-pearl and looks valuable. 'From a Japanese client who's planning to move to Berlin,' I told my wife, although I had no idea whether the abalone sea snail, also known as a sea ear, had any connection to Japan—and why should I have a Japanese client? I never had Japanese clients. Rebecca was pleased and asked no questions.

I had been eating out alone for a while. It started at a time when I could still call my marriage happy. I'd be behind on a commission and forced to put in late nights. If I didn't feel like ordering the usual pizza or Asian takeaway, I'd go and sit in the trattoria around the corner from the office and work on my sketches. Sometimes I took my laptop along. My wife was sympathetic; she appreciated that I couldn't keep on top of my work without sacrificing the odd evening. Soon I was fed up with the food at the trattoria, because the menu never changed and the owner wasn't Italian in any case—he was a Bulgarian playing at being Italian. Nothing against Bulgarians, but if I go out for Italian, I want to see Italians. I want them to say *prego* and *grazie* and, if they insist, *grazie dottore*, even though I don't have a PhD. The Bulgarian said all that, pleasantly enough and with an Italian-sounding accent, but once I'd found out that he was Bulgarian, I began to look around for another restaurant, a better one, and then for an even better one, until I had developed into a connoisseur. It was an expensive business—too expensive, in fact—but I didn't care. I didn't tell my wife where I spent my evenings. She thought I was in the office or at the cheap Italian place around the corner from the office. She was, however, surprised at the speed with which our money was disappearing.

I avoided her at home, too. When I got back from work, I didn't join her in the kitchen where she was peeling carrots or potatoes; I went to the children's rooms. This was easy to justify, because the children hadn't seen their father all day, and children need a father, of course they do. That really is true, but for me the children were also—and these are bitter words—a shield protecting me from being alone with my wife. I looked at her, if I looked at her at all, without being touched by her beauty, and I listened to her, if I listened to her at all, without hearing her words. What drove me away? What drove me away from the woman I had once loved so much?

I know that *I don't know* is not a good answer, but it's the only way I can begin. There is something inexplicable about my retreat, something vague and imprecise. It happened imperceptibly, gradually; I faded away without meaning to, without cause. I simply stayed away. To begin with, it didn't even feel as if that's what I was doing. Our phones make it so easy to distance ourselves from one another without losing touch. I was pleased when I got a loving text message from my wife between courses at Luna or Stranz, or as I was staring with a degree of resentment at a bill for two hundred and fifty euros, not including service, of course, so in fact two hundred and seventy euros—no good being stingy. I would write Rebecca a loving text message back. I wasn't lonely— no one with a family is ever lonely, not even when he's alone, because he knows he can go home to his loved ones at any time. In such circumstances, solitude can become a pleasure.

Now and then I didn't go straight home after dinner, but dropped into a bar and drank a negroni. Sometimes I'd tell the barman about my family—my marvellous children and my beautiful, intelligent and wonderful wife—and because I didn't want the barman wondering why I wasn't with this beautiful, intelligent and wonderful wife, I'd say I lived in Frankfurt—business trip to Berlin, miss her like anything. Ping, a text message. *Sooo tired. Enjoy your work, my poor husband, and give me a kiss when you come to bed, eh?* 'That's her. She's going to bed now,' I'd tell the barman as he mixed me another negroni, and we'd both smile.

'Indestructible' was a word I liked to use on such occasions. 'We have our problems too,' I'd say—to barmen, to my friends, to acquaintances. 'We have our little ups and downs. Don't we all? But one thing's for sure—our marriage is indestructible.' It's a powerful word—a word that speaks of absolute unity, of eternity. How foolish it is to label a marriage with a word like that, particularly in this day and age, when people come together, do what they feel like doing, drift apart, and it's all fine. Marriage is no longer sacrosanct.

The old conventions have broken down, and we have to manage on our own.

Rebecca and I didn't manage very well. When I got home, I would speak more softly, stoop a little. I was smaller, slower, an unassuming person, largely without feelings. It was as that person that I walked through the front door—a hug, a few routine words with my wife, then I'd go to the children's rooms. Even once Paul and Fay were in bed, I didn't talk to my wife; I would sit and read a book. Another evening would pass without conversation, but we were still there, I told myself. Still indestructible. I reassured myself with that powerful and fearful word in those moments of clarity when I realised my marriage was dying a slow death.

9

I AM THE SILENT TYPE, a man who doesn't mind if he doesn't speak or hear a word for days on end, as I realise whenever I'm on one of my thinking retreats: five days on Amrum, walks on the mud flats and in the dunes, intense thinking, sketching in cafes and restaurants, brief exchanges with waiters—not a word too many. I am at ease with myself. I used to think I was probably the only person I could be with without ever getting bored. I also liked to think that the only conversations free from misunderstanding are conversations with oneself. I got positively drunk on such insights. What a fool I was.

The truth is, no one is ever bored in my wife's company. She is more intelligent than me or anyone I know, talkative and original, with a sunny, calm disposition and a good sense of humour, and everything about her is softly elegant, right down to her gliding walk. When I am sitting at home at my desk, Rebecca can startle me by coming up behind me and laying a hand on my shoulder. I don't hear her approaching, although she likes to wear high-heeled shoes even in the flat—and we have parquet floors. It's true that I can become very engrossed in my work, but what other woman can walk across parquet in high heels almost soundlessly? Someone once said of the poet Anna Akhmatova, 'She doesn't touch the ground when she walks...' My wife's like that.

She has rather an unfortunate voice, quite high and inclined to crack, but it doesn't usually matter. Our everyday disagreements aren't that bad—they're mostly arguments rather than fights—and are soon resolved. 'Randolphrandolphrandolph,' says Rebecca, when everything important has been said and anything else would only send us spiralling into destructive loops—and she shakes her head. 'Rebeccarebeccarebecca,' I say, already smiling and in the same tone of reproach and forgiveness—and I too shake my head. Or else I say 'Rebeccarebeccarebecca' first, and then she says 'Randolphrandolphrandolph'. That conciliatory echo never fails us—we can rely on each other for that.

But I am afraid there's a bit more to it than these day-to-day disagreements. My marvellously calm and sunny wife sometimes loses control completely, exploding like a suicide bomber. The comparison is tasteless, but somehow also apposite, because during these fits all traces of Rebecca's usual delightful self are obliterated and the incendiary force of her anger obliterates me too, if only momentarily. I cannot say precisely what triggers these explosions—it is usually funny little things.

For instance, I once announced that I was going to leave for a business trip to Munich on the evening of 1 January, because I had an appointment early the following day. I didn't think Rebecca would mind—New Year's Day is always a write-off, after the party the night before. You sit out your hangover, watch the ski jumping on TV, wonder whether to bother putting your resolutions into practice and go to bed early. On 1 January everyone is as taciturn and self-absorbed as I am on a normal day. No one feels like chatting, or spending time with their family. But when Rebecca heard of my plan, she was furious. She leapt out of her chair, arm outstretched, index finger stabbing at the air. How could I think of abandoning my family during the holidays? Were there no limits? She was shrieking at me, almost screaming, her face red, thick veins protruding from her neck. I could tell just by looking at her there was no point in arguing.

I have to confess, these fits knock me sideways. I freeze, muscles clenched, heart beating wildly, and my head feels as if my brain might explode. I am, I fear, scared at such moments. I want to run away, but I can't move, want to say something but can't speak. Outwardly I am turned to stone, but inside I am raging.

It is only by destroying something that Rebecca can get control of her fury. She hurls a glass at the floor, a plate against the wall. She used to take oranges from the fruit bowls in the kitchen or living room and fling them so hard at the wall that they burst. That proved particularly expensive, because we like to keep our flat looking nice and always had the wallpaper or paint touched up afterwards by professional decorators. We have stopped buying oranges now. As soon as Rebecca has smashed or broken something, she calms down and takes me in her arms, holding me tight and yet lovingly, and stroking my head. 'Sorry,' she whispers in my ear. It takes me a while to ease myself out of my spasm. Then I tell her all is forgiven and help her gather up the broken pieces.

These fits are not frequent, maybe two or three a year. We have sometimes talked about them. Rebecca doesn't know what gets into her any more than I do, or how she can avoid it. We have agreed that I will have to put up with it.

'Can you?' she once asked.

'Of course,' I said, kissing her, but there is no denying that I occasionally feel tense when I am sitting with my wife and things are less than harmonious, or that I may act more than usually charming to avoid triggering a fit. I don't much like myself at such times.

'Her fits are driving me away from her,' I said to my little brother, as we sat together at the counter in Blum, a little old bar near Winterfeldplatz where we always go when he's in Berlin.

'It's not her fault—it's yours,' he said.

'But why does she have to attack me like that?' I asked.

'Because you're starving her.'

'I wouldn't be starving her if she didn't attack me like that,' I told him.

'Stop it,' said my little brother. 'Just try not disappearing for once.'

'I don't disappear,' I said, defiantly.

'Oh yes, you do,' he said. 'It was just the same when we were little. We'd all be there in the living room together, and Mum would sit at the table with us, playing a game, and you'd just disappear.'

'That was Dad's fault,' I said. 'I hated being in the same room as him.'

Then my brother said those words I can't stand: 'You're just like him.' That isn't true—and if it were, I wouldn't want it pointed out to me.

I pushed the flat of my hand against my brother's shoulder, not very hard, but not gently, either. He did the same to me, only rather harder. My negroni, which I was holding in my left hand, sloshed onto my trousers. I put it down, leapt to my feet and pulled my little brother off his stool; two of his shirt buttons burst. We wrestled, but only briefly, because the barman thrust himself between us.

'You'd better clear out of here,' he said.

We paid and left. Outside we laughed about it, hugged each other and set out to find another bar. We drank negronis until dawn.

When I got up at about midday, my little brother was sitting in the kitchen with my wife, drinking coffee while she sewed the buttons back on his shirt.

'You don't have to tell *him* we can't escape our gene pool,' I said ill-naturedly to my wife, who was always telling me precisely that. 'It's what he thinks anyway.'

'Now, now,' said my little brother.

I was still standing in the kitchen door. My wife put down the shirt, button, needle and thread, got up and took me in her arms.

'I love your gene pool,' she said.

I put my right hand on her hip. My little brother got up, came over to us, took my left hand and put it on my wife's shoulder.

'There,' he said, 'you see.'

10

IN THE WEEKS BEFORE DIETER TIBERIUS STRUCK,
Rebecca and I lived together in an almost unbearable state of
apathy. My wife had given up fighting for me. She no longer
asked: 'What's wrong with you?' She always got the same
answer in any case: 'Nothing.' It's the most terrible answer
of all. It ought to be banned, proscribed under the marriage
act, because it's almost never true and leaves the other person
helpless. You can't do anything about nothing.

I lived in the expectation that our conversations would

go awry, and they did go awry. We'd got into a routine of letting it happen—or rather, I'd got into a routine. That meant that my expectations were invariably fulfilled, which is something you can get used to.

One of the peculiarities of our marriage was that we were having amazing sex at that time. Or perhaps I should say that *I* was having amazing sex—but it was a while before that became clear to me. I completely lost myself to my wife's body, terrified but elated, because there was no ground beneath me, no purchase. I'm a talker in bed, a little on the vulgar side, to be honest, but I'm also prone to confessions of eternal love—to declaring *never before* and *never again* and *no other woman*. I kept this up even in our more difficult times, and what I said was perhaps true not only in the moment, while we were in bed, but also more broadly—yet after my violent release I thought no more about it.

About a week before I flew to Bali, my wife flung a question into my post-coital oblivion: 'Who were you sleeping with just now?'

'You,' I said, uncomprehending.

'No,' she said, 'you weren't having sex with the woman you ignore during the day.'

'I never think of anyone else,' I said, and it was the truth. I had no affairs, no fantasies. 'Do you think I'm having an affair?' I asked Rebecca.

'No,' she said, 'I don't think you're having an affair.'

I turned over and laid a hand on her back. 'Not only do I not think of any other woman, there's no other woman I could be thinking of. The evenings I'm not here, I really am alone,' I said, rather moved by my own decency.

'I know,' said Rebecca.

'How do you know?' I asked.

She had followed me, she said, last week, and she had seen me at Luna.

'You were spying on me?' I said indignantly.

She had wanted to know why she no longer interested me, she said, and so one evening she had followed me, and she had seen her husband in an expensive restaurant, sitting alone, surrounded by tables of couples, and this solitary man, her husband, had very slowly lifted a fork holding a piece of sausage to his mouth, gazing at this sausage as if he were contemplating a glorious flower—and then the sausage had vanished into his mouth and he had closed his eyes and chewed the sausage with an expression of rapture. Rebecca really did keep saying 'sausage', and it was true, the third course at Luna that evening had been homemade veal chipolata with Swiss chard and black truffles.

A sad image appeared before me: my wife, in her tan trench coat, standing at the window of Luna, watching her husband feasting in solitary splendour. I imagined it raining, to make it even sadder, but I don't know whether it really did rain that evening.

'Do you know what happened next?' asked Rebecca, my hand still resting on her back. 'After you had eaten your sausage, you took your phone and sent me a text: *Still working, love and kisses.*' She was crying now.

'It was the truth,' I said. 'I was still sketching drafts.'

'I'm sure you were,' she said gently. 'I'm sure you were. But still,' she went on, 'I don't know what's worse—seeing you there with another woman or seeing you there on your own.'

'I'm sorry,' I said.

She sat up. Her index finger shot out at me. 'Oh yes, I do,' she said, her voice tight and shrill. 'I know what's worse. Seeing that empty chair opposite you, because you'd rather have an empty chair than me.' My heart started racing. 'If there had been a woman sitting there with tits and an arse,' Rebecca shrieked, 'for all I care, the best tits and arse in the world, then I could fight against that woman. But I can't fight against an empty chair. I don't know how to fight against an empty chair.' She snatched up the alarm clock that stood on the bedside table and dashed it against the wall.

'Mama?'

Fay was standing in the door, a toy sheep in her arms. Rebecca leapt out of bed, ran to her and lifted her onto her hip. I watched the two of them disappear and then heard whispering and singing. My wife sings nicely, in spite of her high voice.

A quarter of an hour later, Rebecca returned, got into bed

and pressed herself firmly against me, twining her fingers in my hair.

'You don't have sex with me,' she said, after a while, and her voice was calm. 'You have sex with yourself. You go into raptures over yourself and you use me as an instrument.'

'That's not true,' I said, appalled.

'Sssh,' said Rebecca. 'I mean a beautiful instrument, a Stradivarius violin, something very noble and precious. You use me the way a master violinist uses his violin—passionately, lovingly, tenderly. You're very tender. But if it were another woman lying here, you'd get just as carried away, because it's about you, not about the woman.'

I went to protest, but Rebecca put a finger to her lips. 'Sssh,' she said again, and then: 'We must sleep now.'

I lay awake for a long time that night. I tried to think of something that would prove my wife wrong, but didn't come up with much. In the morning I asked her whether she didn't like sex with me, and she said: 'Oh, yes, I like sex with you—it's nice to be present.'

I went to the office in a bad mood, but it didn't last long. There was so much to reassure me. At least the sex was good. At least our holidays and Christmas parties were a success. At least I loved my wife, or at any rate, I could say I did. At least the four of us made a good family—and we really did. We were, without exception, cheerful around the children. They noticed nothing of my drifting away.

The trouble with a long marriage is that there are so many different versions of it. If I wanted to believe that everything between us was fine, I could look back on the good times and tell myself it was true. If I wanted to justify avoiding my wife, I could look back on the not-so-good times, choose a different story, a different version, and still believe it. I told myself what I needed to hear and made no move to change anything.

My wife calls this the privilege of the Anyway World: 'We're your family. We're always here. You have us without making an effort, because we're here anyway. It's lucky for you, but bad luck for us, because there's no pressure on you to change anything. I ought to break up the Anyway World, ought to leave you or start an affair, but I don't want to—I'm your wife.'

I was moved by such words and resolved to change something at last, to come out of my isolation. It was a resolution I often made. I'm the kind who's always giving things up, who likes saying, 'Just once more,' or 'This is the last time.' I have said it to myself at Luna, at Hedin, at Stranz. Time and again I've said to myself, 'One last feast, and then I'll spend all my evenings with Rebecca.' Not long afterwards, I'd be sitting there again, in self-indulgent solitude. Unhappy marriage as a satisfying way of life—maybe that exists.

11

WHEN I LEFT FOR BALI, my wife didn't drive me to the airport, because she had to take our children to some unspecified event. A kiss in the hall, a fleeting hug, Fay cried. I immediately resolved never to travel without my family again. But as it was going to be my last trip without them, I was determined to make the most of it and to some extent I shook off my guilty feelings during the flight. There wasn't much point in doing otherwise. I didn't give a thought to Dieter Tiberius.

My friend Stefan picked me up at Denpasar Airport. We had known each other since our late teens, which is to say, for a long time. Both of us had refused to do the compulsory six months in the military, and instead did national service as civilians, working in an old people's home. Stefan had studied business afterwards and gone to work for Deutsche Bank in Jakarta, where he married an Indonesian woman. Now he was self-employed and involved in complex financial transactions I couldn't fathom, but we usually talked about other things. We were radically open with one another on the subject of our private lives and called this 'talking vulvar', a term we'd coined in our student days, when we would exchange notes on our girlfriends' most intimate body parts. These days we more often talked vulvar about our marital problems, which we divulged in a spirit of rigorous self-examination, but the drive from Denpasar to Seminyak was too short to get started on that. We brought each other up to date on our lives instead and talked about the wedding, his second—another Indonesian woman.

There were three days until the wedding. I was staying at a hotel on the beach and would sleep until midday, read William Faulkner's *Light in August* on my balcony for a couple of hours, do a bit of sketching, go for a spin around Seminyak on a moped I'd hired and then, at about four, head down to the water, where most of the wedding guests had already gathered. It was a broad, white beach—high waves, heat even in the late afternoon. I hired a short surfboard and swam out a little way to wait for some decent waves, but there weren't many. We drifted in the sea, telling each other about our jobs and families, and when a good wave came, we tried to catch it as it broke, throwing our bodies onto the surfboards, paddling briefly with our arms and letting the wave carry us to the beach. It was easy and good fun, and we laughed like children. Later somebody would fetch beer. We hoped for a dramatic sunset, but a grey strip of cloud settled itself between sea and sky every time, and the sun scornfully vanished behind it.

Every afternoon at half past four, groups of twenty or thirty Indonesians descended on the beach, alarming some of the guests. They were festively attired in turbans and brightly coloured scarves, and they sang. They had bowls of blossom with them and long objects that looked like big Christmas crackers. At five o'clock they got up, walked slowly to the water and threw in the things they had brought with them. Then they turned back. The sea washed the things onto the shore again even before these people had left the beach, but they didn't appear to care.

Two or three men from the wedding party said it was a ritual to appease the sea—apparently there had been a tsunami warning. Stefan said that was nonsense. His friends—who did not live in Asia but claimed to have read a lot about it—stood their ground. Some believed them, others didn't. I walked down to the water for a closer look. I found orange-coloured blossoms, woven amulets with gold ribbons, dishes made of palm leaves. I also found a chicken's egg in a plastic bag but didn't know whether it was one of the cult objects or had fallen prey to the sea on some other occasion. I was inclined to disbelieve the alarmists, but I wasn't sure.

Dogs fought on the beach, a few boys played football, and sometimes vendors came by trying to sell us kites in the shape of ships. Some of them hung above us in the sky; they had black sails. I bought a kite for my children. I made an effort to talk to as many of the guests as possible, so no one could comment that I never had anything to say. I was somewhat apprehensive about the speech I had prepared for the wedding reception.

On the second evening we went to Métis, a restaurant-cum-lounge, open on one side and looking out onto long ponds covered with waterlilies. Fat koi swam in and out between the lily pads. A DJ was spinning records, and a trumpeter accompanied the music live. We sat in armchairs, looking at the waterlilies and drinking strawberry mojitos or Moscow mules, our clothes sticking to our skin. I had a long chat with a woman based in Bangkok who was the EU diplomat in charge of Myanmar. She was wearing a short, white, Mondrian-style dress and told me about the generals, and the opposition leader Aung San Suu Kyi in her lakeside house. We flirted a little, aimlessly, only because it was that kind of an evening, and then Stefan joined us. The diplomat left, and we talked vulvar. I told my friend all about Dieter Tiberius and was rather put out when he asked whether, given the circumstances, it was right to leave my family in Berlin. On the other hand, asking uncomfortable questions was precisely the point of our conversations. I said that Tiberius had never been physically threatening and that I didn't consider him dangerous. Later, I lost myself to the trumpet, and it seemed to me I had never heard music that penetrated so deep into my being, but I expect the cocktails were to blame.

At one in the morning it began to rain, and the trumpet was drowned out by the patter. We waited for taxis that were a long time coming. Some of the wedding guests went on to a club; I went back to my hotel and rang my wife. She didn't pick up. She must have been at home—in Germany it was eight in the evening, our children's bedtime. If I had been there, I'd have been reading them a story. In those days I lived a lot in the hypothetical subjunctive. I was often away and would imagine in detail what I would have been doing if I had been with my family. That way, I was half there—in my mind, at any rate—and that reassured me.

Suddenly I began to worry, thinking of Dieter Tiberius. I rang again and left a voice message. 'I love you,' I said at the end. The next morning Rebecca had left me a message in return. She said the children were well and so was she.

On the day before the wedding, my friend had a stag party. He set off with the men, his fiancée with the women. We ate in a restaurant that served gigantic spare ribs, sawing the meat off the bones with sharp knives and then picking them up and gnawing them. We drank beer in a few bars and ended up in a club famous for a drink containing hallucinogenic mushrooms. I had never tried drugs, hadn't even smoked a joint, but I drank out of the glass that was doing the rounds. There were eight of us. Clinging to the wall was a gecko, and somebody said that geckos didn't have eyelids, so they had to moisten their eyes with their tongues—that was why geckos' tongues flickered in and out. I gave a loud laugh. Three women came and stood by our table and danced to the music coming from the speakers—spare, graceful movements. They were Balinese women, small, dainty and young; they wore high-heeled shoes and leopard-skin bikinis, and they danced for us for five minutes. Half an hour later they came back. They were lovely. I looked at them. I felt happy. Then I forgot about them. I didn't notice much effect from the mushrooms.

We decided to meet up with the women guests and carry on partying at Stefan's house. As I was sitting on my moped waiting for the others, one of the dancers came and stood beside me. She was now wearing jeans and a white T-shirt, her long hair tied back in a red band. She smiled at me. I smiled back, shy and a little helpless. I didn't know what she wanted. The others got on their mopeds, ready to set off. As I started up the engine, the Balinese woman got on the pillion seat. I let it happen—that's the only way of putting it. I hadn't asked her to get on, not with words or gestures. I could reproach myself for smiling, but I don't believe there's anything that says you're not allowed to smile. She put her arms around my hips and her hands on my belly and snuggled up to me. We drove through the night until we found the women guests. They too got on their mopeds and followed us. On the way we stopped off at a shop and bought beer, wine, vodka, crisps and chocolate. The Balinese woman asked me my name and then practised saying 'Randolph' until she pronounced it well. She was called Putu.

Stefan lived in a house in the hills above Seminyak. It was open on one side, like most houses in Bali, and the kitchen opened onto the pool. We sat at the kitchen counter, drinking, eating nibbles and laughing. Two of the men were pretty far gone on the mushrooms. They started throwing the women into the pool and then went sailing in themselves. Soon almost everyone was in the water. I didn't resist for long. Two other men, the biggest and heaviest, fought on the lawn beside the pool like elephant bulls until they, too, splashed into the water together. Putu, who had been spared, brought our drinks to the pool. We prattled away, drinking and looking up into the starless sky. Somebody said: 'Let the Asians control the world. Who cares, as long as we get to control the swimming pools?' Everybody laughed.

Later we borrowed clothes from Stefan and his fiancée. Some fitted better than others. A woman from the Goethe Institut swung around the pole of a parasol and claimed it was pole dancing. Then Stefan danced with the pole and managed to poke it into the kitchen fan. The fan stopped for a moment but then continued to turn lopsidedly. We laughed and laughed. I sat in a deckchair, Putu asleep on the lawn beside me. It was six in the morning, and I wondered whether to take her to my room.

At half past six—it was getting light—my phone rang. Everyone started—so many people these days have that ringtone that sounds like an old-fashioned telephone. Most of the guests looked around for their mobiles, some of them realising only now that they had fallen in the water with their phones on them. Loud swearing. The ringing stopped. Soon afterwards it started up again. I heaved myself out of my deckchair—it's not so easy to get out of them at my age—and went to the kitchen counter, where I had left my phone when it had become clear there was no escaping the water. The screen was illuminated, my wife's name flashing across it. In Germany it was half past midnight.

'Hello,' I said, in what I hoped was an unpartyish way.

My wife's voice was panicked. 'Tiberius is in our garden.'

12

I OFTEN WONDERED LATER why the call had to reach me just then. I would have preferred a more appropriate moment, preferred not to be caught in such frivolous circumstances. But is there an appropriate moment for disaster? We can't live our entire lives in such a way that if disaster strikes we can be sure of our dignity—that would be ridiculous. But I'm getting ahead of myself, getting off track. I shouldn't do that. And why am I constantly defending myself? I really ought to stop.

Rebecca had already rung the police. She had gone to bed early, hadn't been able to sleep, and after a while she had got up to have a drink of water. Our kitchen is at the back of the house, and when my wife looked out at the garden as she drank the water, she saw a figure in the moonlight behind a birch tree. My wife couldn't be seen, because she hadn't switched on the kitchen light. The figure moved away from the birch and she saw that it was Dieter Tiberius, who now ran across the garden to our house and up the steps to our conservatory. At the top, he leaned over the railings and peered in at our daughter's bedroom window. He was sweating profusely. He ran back, hid behind the birch, then set off again, once more staring through Fay's window. My wife rang the police, then me.

'Where's Tiberius now?' I asked.

'Behind the compost heap,' said my wife.

'Get the breadknife,' I said.

'I've already got the breadknife,' said my wife.

'Are all the doors locked?' I asked, helplessly.

'Of course,' said my wife, and then added, 'I'm scared.'

'Why aren't the police there yet?' I asked.

'Now he's running across the garden,' she said. 'He keeps running backwards and forwards—what's he doing?'

'Jesus, where are the police?' I cried.

Then there was silence.

'What the fuck's going on?' I yelled into the phone.

'Where is he?'

'I can't see him anymore,' said my wife. I heard our doorbell. 'That's the police,' said my wife.

'Ring me back,' I said.

'Okay,' she said and hung up.

I turned around and saw the remains of the wedding party. I saw the empty bottles, the half-empty bags of crisps, the pool, the sleepy people in deckchairs—among them the woman who knew Aung San Suu Kyi—and Putu, who had woken up and was smiling at me. Stefan came over and asked what had happened. I told him and said I would get myself a return flight immediately. He understood, of course, and asked if he could help in any way.

'Can you make sure the girl gets home?' I asked.

'Sure,' he said.

We hugged, and I glanced at Putu, who looked back questioningly. Then I went to find my moped and drove it through the waking town, down to the hotel.

I rang my wife as soon as I arrived, but she said the police were still there and she'd be in touch later. I packed my things, checked out and got someone to take me to the airport.

Rebecca rang and told me that the police had cautioned Dieter Tiberius.

'Cautioned?' I asked. 'Is that all?'

'Yes, that's all,' she said.

'Isn't it trespassing, at least?' I wanted to know.

'No,' she said. 'He didn't try to get into our flat.'

I didn't understand. As I saw it, he had besieged our house; surely that was a punishable offence.

'How about stalking?' I asked. 'He's a stalker—surely there are procedures for dealing with them?'

I heard our doorbell again and my wife said Mathilde had arrived, her best friend. Mathilde was going to spend the rest of the night with her, she said, as there was no way she could stay alone in the flat with the children. I thought she put a strange emphasis on the word 'alone', but I wasn't sure.

I told her I would try to get a quick flight back. I was going to say a whole lot more, but she had already pressed the buzzer that opened the front door and I could hear her friend's voice.

'Bye,' said my wife and hung up.

I booked flights back to Berlin via Singapore and Paris, mainly with Singapore Airlines. There was only one seat left in business class. Take-off was at 6.05 pm—not for another eight hours. I sat in Starbucks in the departure lounge, drinking espresso after espresso, regretting everything I had done over the past two months, and above all what I had not done: put Dieter Tiberius in his place, been with my family. I regretted the trip to Bali, and bringing Putu back with me from the bar. What had I been thinking? But nothing had actually happened—that was something.

I thought about what I would do now: consult our lawyer,

go and see Tiberius's landlord, approach the police. He had to move out of the basement. There was no other way—no question of reconciliation, of coming to an agreement. We couldn't live under the same roof as that man. I googled 'stalking' on my phone and read my way through a number of websites. The problem, it seemed, was that you couldn't do anything about it unless the stalker became violent. I was despondent at first, then cautiously optimistic again, telling myself that there was no way Tiberius could get away with it, not in a country where the rule of law prevailed.

In the early afternoon I rang my wife, and she cried. She hadn't slept. I told her everything I was going to do and that we'd soon be rid of that bastard. My wife said she was taking the children to stay the night at her friend's. Then I talked to Paul and Fay and said what I always said when I was away: that I missed them and that I'd soon be back and we'd go to the zoo. My voice cracked, and I had tears in my eyes.

On the short flight from Denpasar to Singapore, I slept.

When we landed, I immediately switched my phone on and waited impatiently for it to find a network. There were two voicemail messages from my wife. *Call me urgently*, and then: *Why haven't you called?*

I called her straight away, and she told me that Dieter Tiberius had left a letter on the doormat, three pages, handwritten. It said he had suspected for some time now that we were sexually abusing our children, so he had started to watch us from the garden at night and was in possession of evidence that he would be handing over to the police.

I laughed. 'Now we've got him,' I said. 'If he's spouting that sort of filth, we'll soon have him out of the house.'

'But what if the police believe him?' said my wife.

'They won't believe him,' I said. 'That's absurd.' Then my phone died.

I had a two-hour wait before my flight to Paris and spent the first part of it looking for a shop that sold adaptors for the electrical sockets in Singapore. I had a universal adaptor that fitted pretty much every socket in the world but had stupidly packed it in my suitcase—so much for my status as a global traveller.

I hurried along the rows of shops—perfume, clothes, electrical appliances, alcohol, all the big brand names—and at last I found an adaptor, but then I couldn't find anywhere to plug it in. Finally I went into the men's toilets and plugged my phone into a shaving socket to charge. Men came and went. I heard them urinate, some of them with a sigh. They washed their hands beside me, their tired eyes in the mirrors. One man gave me a surprised look. What did he see? A child abuser?

My relief had evaporated. 'What if the police believe him?' my wife had asked. It was not impossible—they were highly sensitive to the possibility of child abuse these days, and rightly so. Then a film unspooled in my head, a film I have seen a thousand times since, as sharp and vibrant as on the big screen. Only it wasn't on the big screen—it was all in my mind.

It began with a tracking shot of a suburb—strangely, or perhaps not so strangely, an American suburb, because almost all the films we see are American, so when we think of ourselves as characters in a film, we always imagine ourselves in American towns and landscapes. It was one of those clean suburbs where all the houses look the same: tidy, with well-kept lawns, and middle-of-the-range cars parked in the drive. The terrible thing about suburbs like that is that in the midst of all this sameness, any deviation sticks out like a sore thumb. Decent people live there, and anyone less than decent stands out.

The camera comes to a halt outside one of the houses, peeps in at the window and sees cheerful everyday life, wholesome and intact. A family is sitting having breakfast: a beautiful woman, a respectable, hardworking man, two delightful children. It is us. The stalker appears. He slinks around the house, a sinister fellow: ugly, down at heel, an evil villain, bent on the destruction of all that is good and pure. To begin with, the family appears inviolable, but there is a twist in the plot: an overzealous social worker, a corrupt lawyer, a disreputable journalist, a malevolent public. At the end, the children are in state care, their father is in prison, and their mother is walking the streets in order to survive.

The last shot is of the house at dusk, a sign on the lawn: *For Sale*. The lie in this film was 'wholesome and intact'. My family was not neither wholesome nor intact.

My mobile had some juice again—it could, at least, be switched on—and I rang my wife and told her we weren't child abusers, that everybody knew that and that we had nothing to be afraid of.

'Where are you?' my wife asked.

'In the men's toilets,' I said.

'Why are you ringing me from the men's toilets?' Rebecca asked. I explained that my phone's battery was flat and I couldn't use it without a power connection.

'Don't be scared,' I implored her, and a man looked at me, probably a German. 'I'll ring again in ten minutes,' I said.

I hung up, and waited and waited until the phone was slightly recharged again. I pulled out the plug, stowed everything away in my bag, rushed out and rang my wife. She didn't pick up the landline at home, and I couldn't get hold of her on her mobile either. I walked around the airport and back past the luxury shops as if in a trance, listening to the loudspeaker announcements: flights to Kuala Lumpur, Bangalore, Melbourne, Los Angeles, Phnom Penh.

I had been to Singapore once, three years ago, when Stefan was working there. We had been to a big dinner at Raffles Hotel, and before long I had felt disgruntled at the way all the Europeans, all the citizens of western democracies gathered there, seemed to feel so very much at home in Singapore. The family of Lee Kuan Yew had ruled with a rod of iron for decades, and those who broke the law faced draconian punishments—canings and executions—but throughout the main course I heard nothing but praise for the city's order and security. Now, waiting in the departure lounge for the Singapore Airlines flight to Paris, I thought: *If this has to happen to me, why can't it happen in Singapore? They'd know how to deal with Tiberius here. The death penalty.* This thought was, if I remember rightly, my next step towards barbarism.

I didn't sleep on the flight to Paris. I went to the toilet three times to listen to my voicemail, because I was afraid I might have had a phone call from the child welfare office. But there was nothing. I watched three films without sound—a Woody Allen film, a Clint Eastwood and one of the Harry Potters; I forget which—and I kept an eye on the little aeroplane that was making its way across the screen towards Paris. In my head, my American film unspooled, interspersed with desolate thoughts of what I would do to Dieter Tiberius as soon as I laid hands on him: fractured nose, massive bruising everywhere. A moment later, I was once again the model citizen of a model state where the rule of law prevailed. We had acted lawfully and we would continue to act lawfully, so the law would protect us. Dieter Tiberius could start to pack his bags.

Charles de Gaulle, yet another airport—more loathing of airports, more disconsolate waiting. Then Berlin. My wife was there with Paul and Fay at the arrivals gate—big hugs such as we hadn't given each other for a long time, hugs that had no history, that knew nothing of the last years of our marriage. Desperate hugs. In the car on the way home I told the children about the sky ships with the black sails, and the dogs on the beach. Our house stood white in the morning sun, quiet and peaceful. Nothing stirred. It was the house I knew and yet it was utterly different.

13

I THINK I'M UNLUCKY WITH HOUSES, with property. When we were tenants in a sixth-floor flat on the estate, all was well with me. My troubles only began when we moved into our own place—although even then they didn't begin immediately.

We moved early in 1973, when I had just turned ten. I remember hardly anything of the next few years—nothing personal at any rate. Of course I know where I watched the '74 World Cup final—at the Wacker 04 clubhouse, with meatballs and lemonade to celebrate Germany's victory. I also remember Willy Brandt resigning as chancellor after one of his closest aides was exposed as a Stasi intelligence agent. My father said the aide should be put up against the wall, and it made sense to me: he was a spy, and the spies in my books often met just such an end.

My father's guns were not something we talked about. They were simply there, and we accepted that as normal. All the same, I was aware that other fathers did not leave the house with guns tucked beneath their armpits. At first, I supposed that my father was in charge of security at the dealership, as well as selling cars. But they didn't have large quantities of cash on the premises—it couldn't be that. And so I hit on the notion that he led a second, secret life: he was a killer, or the head of a mafia-type organisation and we, his family, were his cover. Or else he was actually an agent.

Berlin was a city of agents, and the role of my home town in the Cold War had become increasingly clear to me. We were the centre of it all: it was here that the systems came crashing together, ours good and theirs bad. And wasn't Ford an American company that might well provide cover for government agents?

I began to observe my father more closely, but saw nothing to confirm my suspicions. On workdays he left the house at a quarter to eight and was back at a quarter past seven without fail. We would have dinner, and after dinner we sat in the living room, talking and playing games with my mother, while he read on the sofa or cleaned his guns. I shall never forget the smell of Ballistol. On Saturdays he drove to the firing range, but my sister was with him, and on Sundays we walked in the woods.

I paid surprise visits to the dealership to see if he really was always there. He always was, and I never caught him hurriedly seeing off some shady character, or hastily hanging up the phone when he saw me. There had, though, been a change over the years. Potential customers no longer came and marvelled; they came as experts now. They knew all about cars and were not going to let it slip my father's attention. He was no longer king of the Ford dealership—I was aware of that—but that didn't matter if he was an agent, and for a time I had no doubt of that at all. I would have loved to tell my friends that we were not the family they thought we were, not a family like any other—more like a family on TV. But I couldn't mention it. We'd had it drummed into us not to talk about my father's guns, not under any circumstances.

I didn't even tell Klaus Karmoll about the guns—Klaus Karmoll who was older than me, and stronger, and sometimes lay in wait for me on the way to school. I had no means of defending myself and would have loved to tell him we had a Colt at home, a few shotguns and some pistols, including a Walther PPK that I was quite capable of handling. But I said nothing and put up with the beatings, so firm was my belief that disaster would strike if anyone found out about my father's guns. I never had the feeling that weapons made me safer—in fact my father was always afraid that our house would be broken into, or that he himself would be mugged, by gang members in need of guns.

One occasion I do remember from our time in the new house—which is to say, my teenage years—is a Saturday when my father did not drive to the firing range. I was maybe thirteen. I no longer believed my father was an agent—he was, I thought, simply a gun enthusiast. That Saturday he came home in the afternoon laden with bags and parcels, which he put down in the living room, telling us not to touch them. Of course we tiptoed around the enormous pile and soon figured out what he'd bought: a tent, together with a whole host of other things to guarantee survival at six thousand metres. I was thrilled—we were going to set off, at last, my father and I, his travelling companion. The adventures could begin.

At the same time, I was surprised, because my father and I were no longer as close as we had been. In those quiet years between 1973 and 1975, I had somehow lost him. I don't know what happened. We drifted apart so gradually that I can hardly remember it happening. I only know that around 1975, things were no longer right between us. I can't recall any conversations, anything we did together. He hadn't been to any of my football games for years, although I wasn't a bad goalie, nothing for a father to be ashamed of. But he didn't come, not even when Wacker 04 played against Hertha Zehlendorf or Hertha BSC—and those were matches worth watching.

After I turned thirteen he had no further opportunity, because I quit the team. Over time I had developed a strange fear of being alone in the goal. In those days, boys weren't as well trained in tactics as they are today; chances to score were often the result of what I called 'attacks'. My defence would be a long way down the field because they all wanted to play at the front, and then they'd lose the ball and suddenly three players from the opposing team were charging in my direction and there was no one to help me, no purple shirt anywhere near. I couldn't take it anymore and asked to play in another position, but I wasn't talented enough, so I stopped playing at the club altogether.

When I think about it now, I don't remember my father *ever* coming to see me in a match, though I expect he came along now and again when I was little. With no shared interests, we had lost touch with each other—but the mound of camping equipment in the living room seemed to announce a renewed effort on his part. He had bought the gear for the journeys we had once planned, and I was pleased. It would have been even nicer if he had taken me with him to choose the things, but perhaps it was supposed to be a surprise.

I had been asked round to a friend's house that afternoon,

and when I got back in the evening, the tent was in the garden. I went up to it, pulled open the zip and saw one sleeping bag and one thermal mat. My things must be in my room, I thought, but when I checked upstairs there was nothing there.

I went back down to the living room and found my mother playing board games with my brother and sister. My father was there too, reading—a quick hello and he went back to his magazine. I played a round of Chinese chequers, but as nothing was said, I soon took myself off upstairs again, where I ran a bath and then sat in it, brooding. I had no idea what was going on.

When I returned to my room after my soak, wrapped in a towel, I looked into the garden and saw light in the Himalaya-proof tent. Now I was furious, and stormed up the spiral staircase to my sister's room in the attic. She asked in an unfriendly way what I wanted. We didn't get on well.

'Nothing,' I said curtly and went back down.

'Don't come up here again,' she yelled after me.

Cornelia has been dead for several years and today these memories are painful to me. I have a photo of the two of us on my bookcase—my mother gave it to me for my last birthday. The photo is in a gold frame, perhaps twelve by twelve centimetres, and mounted on purple card with a gold-coloured floral pattern. The photo is small—a miniature. My sister is maybe four years old, so I'd be three. She has plaits and is wearing a short dress. I have close-cropped hair and am wearing short trousers. We're holding hands. My sister is half a pace ahead of me, looking cheerful and determined as she leads me through life. I follow, turned in on myself.

'That is the sister I never had,' I said to my wife, as I looked at the photo.

'Maybe it's the sister you had then,' she said.

Her words stunned me. I had never seen it like that. I remembered my sister as the beast I fought for supremacy. We hurt each other so badly that it was years before we finally started to get on—not until we were twenty or twenty-one, and then we liked each other up to a point, but never got properly close, not even just before her death.

I was relieved that my sister wasn't sitting in the tent with my father, that she wasn't going to be his companion—and I was sorry the same was true of me. I couldn't sleep for a long time. I kept getting up, going over to the window and looking down into the garden. I could see the tent lit up from the inside. I could see my father's shadow as he sat there, probably reading *Auto Motor and Sport*, in the light of a high-power torch bright enough to help you find your way to the top of Mount Everest at night in a snowstorm at seven thousand five hundred metres. Later, it was dark down there.

When I woke up in the morning and looked into the garden, the tent was gone. I never saw it again. My father never went on his journeys of adventure, not even by himself.

He never even travelled without his wife, as far as I know, and the furthest they got was Lake Garda in northern Italy, where they stayed in a guesthouse. He was a dreamer who didn't have the nerve to do much, but never stopped thinking that he would. In that respect he was an optimist after all.

14

MY FATHER WAS SOMETIMES IRASCIBLE OR TETCHY, even in my childhood, but during my teenage years he would fall for days into a black mood from which my mother was unable to rouse him. He did nothing but sit on the sofa and sulk. He would explode at the slightest disturbance, so even in our rooms we could only listen to music turned down low, or had to reckon with an irate visit. It once cost me the pick-up of my record-player when my father put a brutal end to a Pink Floyd song.

I don't want to claim that it was solely my father's fault that he and I talked to one another so little—that he barely took any notice of me. I think the most disastrous discovery of my teenage years was that my grammar-school teachers and friends considered me intelligent. My parents aren't stupid, not by any means, but neither of them went to university: my father failed his leaving exams and my mother left school at fourteen, because her parents couldn't afford anything else. I soon began to feel that I was more intelligent than my parents, and I am ashamed to say that I acted in such a way that they couldn't fail to notice. My mother bravely took me on in every debate I forced on her, although I sometimes jeered at her. Whenever I launched into one of these debates at dinner, my father would leave the table and sit on the sofa. He read or cleaned his guns, but I knew he was listening. I knew too that after a while he would jump to his feet and start shouting. At that point, I would go to my room with a smirk, but my heart was pounding. I was seized by the fear that he might come up and shoot me.

By then I was fifteen or sixteen and knew my father was not a spy. I knew too that he was more than just an amateur marksman, a hunter and a gun enthusiast. He needed the guns to protect himself. He was afraid. I didn't know what he was afraid of—as far as I could tell, he had nothing to fear, no reason to be frightened. He didn't hang out in the red-light district in town. He didn't even go to normal pubs, where he might have got into a fight after a few beers. He was almost always at home when he wasn't working. And yet I saw him strap on his holster and put in a gun before he drove to the shops with my mother. What was he so scared of? And why did I never ask? I would love to ask him now, but I can't do it with Kottke around, and Kottke is, by force of circumstance, always around when I visit my father.

I couldn't fail to notice at the time that my father had guns not only to shoot at targets, but also to shoot at people— in case he was threatened, I suppose, for he was not the kind to go about attacking others. He took part in combat training—self-defence courses in small arms fire. I saw him practise at home. He wore a holster at his belt, threw a coin in the air and pulled the gun. He didn't shoot: the idea was to pull the revolver before the five-mark piece fell to the floor. My little brother liked watching him. I went to my room as soon as these drills began.

Bruno is three years younger than me. In the flat on the estate we shared a room. There is a photo that shows him sitting in a big pram, looking into the camera in astonishment. I am standing at the handle of the pram, the big brother. I didn't love him instantly, because I had to make space for him in my small room and because he cried a lot when he was a baby. But I soon set him to gathering up the cars I raced down my magnetic track and bringing them back to me, and in return I let him push a car down the track himself every now and then. I loved him before I had a word for it, and I still love him, although it's not always easy with Bruno.

When we went to the car dealership together, he would run straight to the garage, a place I didn't like, loud and dirty. In those days garages were still oily—today they're more like electronics labs. It made his day when one of the mechanics allowed him to give a screwdriver or monkey wrench a few twists. I preferred to sit in the new cars and pretend to drive. I especially liked the cars with leather seats, because they smelt so tangy.

For a time my father took my little brother along to the firing range, but Bruno does not respond well to rigorous discipline—and discipline, my father said more often than necessary, is what matters most at the firing range. Bruno waved the gun around or annoyed people who were trying to concentrate on their next shot. When he took a pot shot at a bird, my father put an end to his career as a marksman. Only my sister continued to shoot. She was Berlin's vice-champion in some youth class, and the cup stood in our living room; Bruno and I made jokes about it, partly because it pained us to see so much made of Cornelia's shooting skills. I don't know how hard it was on my father to realise that neither of his boys was any good as a marksman, but I am sure that my disappointment in him was matched by his disappointment in me and my little brother.

One evening I was lying on my bed, reading, when I heard a gunshot. I ran downstairs, terrified that my father had killed my little brother. No one made him freak out the way Bruno did—but when I burst into the living room, Bruno was alive and well, sitting at the table with my sister and mother, playing a memory game. My father was wearing his belt holster, standing at the patio door looking at a hole in the windowpane. On the floor lay a five-mark piece. His revolver had gone off inadvertently and we were all lucky that no one was walking past our house when it happened.

Lying on my bed again later, I pondered the fact that the guns my father kept at home were obviously loaded. I had known that he was well equipped with ammunition—the brightly coloured cardboard boxes were sometimes stacked on our dining table—but my father stored guns and cartridges separately, and never brought them out at the same time. He was—I had always believed—very particular about safety.

15

I WANT TO STRESS HERE that even my teenage years were completely normal. That is another trap into which historical narrative can fall: when prominence is given to dramatic events, every era seems eventful, or even turbulent. Our days were calm, especially at home. We got up in the morning and breakfast was ready; we went to school, came home again, did our homework, met up with friends; then, in the evening, we ate dinner with our parents, talking to my mother while my father, as a rule, read peacefully. On rare occasions he would interrupt our conversations to recount an episode from his youth or an incident that had taken place at the car dealership. If he was brooding, we didn't let it bother us. After dinner I usually went to my room to read and listen to music. My sister and brother stayed and played games with our mother. When it was time for Bruno to go to bed, I read him a story, and then we talked a bit before our mother came to say our prayers with us. Silently, I continued to thank the good Lord for my happy life.

But there were also these moments of shock, and there was an underlying fear—fear for myself, but more still for my brother. The wooden coathanger days were a thing of the past—my mother no longer hit us—but we might be grounded, or lose our pocket money, which was also painful, in a way. My little brother still got beaten—but only by my father. When Bruno provoked him, my father lost control.

Once I heard my little brother screaming and immediately ran downstairs, jumping four steps at a time. I saw him sitting on the floor, his arms pressed over his head as my father, blind with rage, rained hard, brutal blows on him. My mother grabbed at his hands, but he kept shaking her off.

'Hermann,' she cried. 'Hermann, stop it!'

When my father saw me, he paused before delivering one last blow.

'I'll...' he snarled.

'Hermann,' my mother cried.

I pulled Bruno up and took him to my room. He threw himself on my bed and sobbed uncontrollably. I sat with him, stroking his head.

'I'm going to kill Dad,' my little brother sobbed. Such words have probably been thought or spoken in many a teenager's room, but they sound different in a house full of guns.

'Calm down, easy does it,' I said, though I was agitated too, afraid that my father had taken a pistol out of the safe in the bedroom he shared with my mother and was on his way to shoot us. I got up and listened at the door—nothing. I locked it.

We set up our slot car racing track and had almost finished when the doorhandle turned. We froze, but then we heard our mother's voice. I unlocked the door, and she came in. We saw at once that she hadn't been crying. Bruno wouldn't let her take him in her arms, so she sat down on the chair at my desk. When you talk to our mother, even after a dreadful scene like this, you always come away feeling that everything's fine, that the world's a lovely place. She glosses over anything that might contradict this point of view. It was just the same this time. She said that Bruno shouldn't provoke his father—said it very gently, almost sympathetically: she thought it would be nice if Bruno could avoid provoking his father in future.

'I didn't say anything,' Bruno protested.

'But you told me I was only my husband's servant,' my mother said, 'and that wasn't kind.'

Bruno had only told me that Dad freaked out because he, Bruno, had been arguing with Mum—and that Dad suddenly threw his newspaper to the floor, leapt up from the sofa and laid into him. He hadn't told me what the argument was about.

'I'm not your father's servant,' my mother said now to Bruno, 'and I was glad to give up my job—for the three of you as well as for him.'

I could imagine Bruno making this accusation, definitely not in the calm tone my mother had just used, and definitely not just once, but over and over again and with growing aggression. He was like that at the time, and I wasn't so very different myself.

'But that's no reason to beat someone half to death,' I said to my mother.

'Your father wouldn't beat you half to death,' my mother said.

'But he did,' cried Bruno.

We now got into a discussion such as we often used to have with our mother. We said that our father was terrible; she said that wasn't true. She always protected him when we spoke badly of him. But she also protected us when he got angry with us. That was her role: to mediate, to appease, to pacify. She did it in a calm, almost relaxed manner, as if things weren't as bad as all that, as if everything were perfectly normal.

I don't know whether she really saw it that way. It's possible. If you walked through the burning city of Cologne as a little girl, heard the bombers, the shells and the sirens, knew the smell of burnt human flesh and had to see open wounds and torn limbs, perhaps you feel that you have put the worst behind you—that a domestic dispute is a trivial matter. But it is also possible that my mother, bombed out of her home and left fatherless by the war, knew too much suffering and loss as a child and can't take any more, so that, no matter what the actual state of the world, she chooses to believe that all is well. Perhaps she told herself that our home was a happy one, despite my father's stockpile of weapons and the threat it posed to her children. On the other hand, perhaps she knew for certain that her children were not even remotely in danger, because she was sure she could trust her husband. I don't know. I must ask her some time. All I know is that my mother always kept her cool. It was no different that evening. She talked to us for half an hour and then said goodnight, as if a sweet, weightless sleep lay ahead of us all, and went back down to her husband. I locked the door again.

Bruno and I raced our cars until midnight. Then I carried Bruno's mattress into my room and put it next to my bed. I soon heard him breathing peacefully, but I lay awake for a long time, wondering what I'd do if my father did show up after all. He had said, 'I'll...' and I could only complete the sentence with '...kill you', although, looking back, I'm sure that wasn't what he meant. It was a quirk of my father's to utter vague threats. 'Just you wait,' he'd say, 'I'll...' In a household like ours, unspoken threats had terrible implications. Although I don't own a gun, it has taught me that I shouldn't be vague when I discipline my children. I have to tell them exactly what to expect if they carry on making mush of their food or throwing tennis balls at the dog to make it howl.

I had long ago thought up strategies for dodging a bullet from one of my father's guns. I had considered putting my mattress up against the door; that might stop the bullets. That night, we even had two mattresses, which would make things better. But of course my father could shoot open the lock, and then he'd be with us in no time. As soon as we heard him, we'd have to make a dash for the window, slide a little way down the roof tiles and drop to the ground, making sure to land on our feet.

The question was whether my little brother should climb out first or me. There were pros and cons. If I were first, he'd be at risk for longer, but I'd be able to catch him at the bottom. I found it hard to make up my mind. In the end I decided it would be better to let him get away first—I thought he'd probably manage the jump. Once on the ground, we would have to start running, zigzagging across the lawn, which provided a superb field of fire, of course, but perhaps the darkness would protect us—clouds, no moon—and at the back of the garden on the right, shrubs were waiting to hide us from our father's view. After that we would be safe, because I didn't believe my father capable of finding us in the surrounding gardens—they were our territory.

Later, much later, during an argument with my little brother at a bar, I told him I'd saved his life that day. It was a stupid thing to say, of course, and not even true. The lines of my brother's mouth instantly hardened, and he said he didn't want a life he owed to my generosity. We had one of our ridiculous fights, but made it up over the beer after next. No doubt about it, the two of us, our parents' surviving children, are scarred. Nothing terrible ever happened to us. My father never shot us, never took aim at us, never even threatened to shoot. We grew up as untouched by weapons as everyone else—but for the fact that the guns were there, which changed everything. It meant there were different possibilities—possible threats, in particular. It changed the way we thought and, looking back, sometimes inclined us towards hysteria. For me, home was a place where you could get shot.

I know what suggests itself at this point: my trouble adapting to a new flat and solitary evenings in starred restaurants might have something to do with the threat I felt in my own home as a teenager. Maybe there's something in that, but on the whole such an interpretation seems to me simplistic. I am not the victim of my father's guns. You could also look at it like this: our childhood was exciting; it was intense. It had its moments.

What strikes me today is not so much the sense of menace at home as my father's fears. I recall one incident that left us all speechless. We had driven to Karstadt department store together, not in the Ford 12M, which was too small by then, but in a Ford Granada.

'We need new winter clothes,' my mother had said, and a little later we were circling around the store's car park. It took us a long while to find a space, although a prize had been offered to the first to spot one—a Nuts bar.

'There! There!' my little brother crowed after some time, to the chagrin of his brother and sister, who were sitting one either side of him.

My father let the Granada roll slowly towards the parking space, but a rally-style Kadett GT/E, yellow on the top and black on the bottom, shot out from the left, cutting us off. We couldn't get past, but the Kadett couldn't park either, unless we moved back—the corner was too sharp. My father had one of his fits of wrath, yelling and flailing his arms about, but the driver of the Kadett, a young man, just grinned insolently. We sat there like that for a while and slowly the fear crept up on me that my father would get out of the car and shoot the man in the Kadett. He had a revolver tucked under his armpit—I had seen it when we were putting our coats on. Then my father went very quiet and I panicked, but he didn't get out—he put his foot down and drove away.

Now I was horrified for a different reason, as were my brother and sister. How could he give up a parking space that was clearly ours? My father was big and strong—he could have seen off that idiot in the Kadett even without his revolver. We didn't look for another parking space—my father turned the Granada around and we drove home in silence. My little brother made a brief attempt to claim his Nuts bar—because he'd discovered the parking space and it wasn't his fault, was it, if my father didn't drive into it, but my sister quickly shut him up, to my relief.

I think that encounter taught me a lot about my father. He couldn't argue, couldn't assert himself with words or gestures—his only options, when faced with a problem, were to run away or shoot. Luckily, he always ran away. I don't know why he was like that. The childhood he described to us was a normal childhood. He was an only child whose parents owned a pub in Spandau, and he saw little of the war because his parents sent him to an uncle's farm in Westphalia when the bombing got bad.

My father said his mother often beat him with the poker, and that his father had been a policeman before opening the pub and had always brought his service weapon home. That weapon had interested him, he said. Later, he had a big fight with his parents because they insisted he take over the pub and he was determined not to. Just as he loved guns, he also loved cars, and so, after failing his school leaving exams, he became a mechanic, though he'd rather have been an engineer. My father didn't do military service: too young during the war, too old afterwards. Are these clues that could help to explain my father's peculiar life? When he comes out of prison, I have a great deal to ask him.

16

WHEN WE GOT HOME after my return from Bali, there was a bulging letter on the windowsill in the common entryway. *For Rebecca Tiefenthaler*, it said on the envelope, and on the back: *Dieter Tiberius.*

'Who's that letter from?' Paul asked.

'Just someone I know,' my wife said blithely.

It was then that we started to put on an act—though my wife had presumably started when I was in Bali. We're generally bright, if not cheerful, in the presence of our

children. We remained that way even while dealing with
Dieter Tiberius and his threats, but from then on it was only
a pretence. That was the first drastic change he imposed on
us: we started acting, and our lives became a performance for
our children.

I was first at the door to our flat. I unlocked it and walked
through all the rooms as if on patrol. It was as it always was.
It was a pleasant day, and the rooms were filled with sun. My
wife locked herself in the toilet, and I knew she would read
the letter there. I went into the kitchen and made breakfast
for the children, telling them about Bali, the sea, the surfing.

'Imagine, Dada on a surfboard,' I said, my throat tight.
They laughed. My wife came back. She'd put the letter away
somewhere so the children wouldn't be reminded of it.

'Dada went surfing,' Fay said.

'That must have looked funny,' my wife said.

'Really funny,' said Paul.

'Dada used to be a world champion in surfing,' I said.

'Wow,' said Fay.

'That's a big fib,' Paul crowed.

I couldn't stop thinking: Dialogue between parents
accused of sexually abusing their children and the children
in question. The awful thing was that Paul and Fay were
in the way right now. I wanted to know what was in the
letter—I had to know—but we couldn't talk about it as long
as they were around.

'Time to leave for kindergarten,' I said, getting up. 'Teeth brushed, jackets on.'

While Rebecca helped the children pack their bags and put on their shoes, I went out to the garage, taking the short cut through the basement. Passing the door to Dieter Tiberius's flat, I pricked up my ears: nothing, not a peep. I kicked the door down and hurled myself at the sleeping man, but only in my head, and then carried on out into the yard.

I retrieved my bike from the garage, then Paul's bike, as if on autopilot, and a moment later my wife appeared with the children. She'd gone round the side of the house, not through the basement.

Then the familiar ritual: children's helmets on, Fay in the child seat, a kiss for my wife.

I hesitated. 'Did you want to come with us?'

'No, it's all right,' she said and kissed the children goodbye.

We cycled to kindergarten. I dropped off Paul and Fay and rushed back. My wife was sitting in the living room, talking to her mother on the phone, the letter on the sofa beside her.

'I'll read you what he's written,' she said when she'd hung up.

'Not here,' I said. 'Let's go in the kitchen.' The basement flat is under our living room. We could hear Dustin Hoffman's voice when we were in there, so Dieter Tiberius could probably hear us too.

We sat down at the kitchen table and my wife read me the letter. It was eleven pages long. Dieter Tiberius gave a detailed account of what my wife and I had, in his opinion, been doing to our children. I can't quote it here, although I remember it precisely, because I was to read the letter many times in the months that followed, with a disgust previously unknown to me. I will only say that most of the scenes that Dieter Tiberius described took place in the bathroom, and some in our bed. Frequent words were 'willy' and 'fanny', and he said that the children shouted, 'Oh, that's hot,' or 'Don't rub so hard.'

I found it particularly upsetting that the account was not wholly the product of a sick imagination, but shot through with real-life detail—the detail of our family life. 'Don't rub so hard' are words that have been said in our bathroom—as are the words 'Oh, that's hot'. They are probably to be heard in all bathrooms the world over where small children get washed. Dieter Tiberius had overheard them being used by our children and incorporated them in his sick fantasies. In this way he deprived us of the sense of pure innocence that his very accusations left us in such sore need of.

Even before my wife had reached the end of the letter, I had begun searching my memory for the situations he described. When had I let the shower run too hot? When had I rubbed too hard with a towel that was a bit too rough? And didn't the jet of too-hot water and the not entirely gentle way

I dried my children in the morning rush constitute minor assaults in themselves? With his letter, Dieter Tiberius had sown in us the seeds of self-doubt, and so it was to continue in the months to come.

My wife put the letter on the kitchen table and said, 'He wants our children.' The same thought had occurred to me—anyone describing sex with children in such detail could only be a paedophile. 'I'll kill him,' Rebecca said, her voice high and unsteady. 'I'll kill him!' She jumped from her seat. 'He's an animal!' she shrieked. 'He's a filthy animal, a freak, a pervert! I'm going to kill him!'

I took her in my arms, and we stood in our kitchen holding each other tight for a long while. I think it was the first time I took my wife in my arms unprompted after one of her screaming fits.

In that moment, I thought all was well between us, that we had had our crisis, but that, in the face of danger, we had weathered it. I was wrong: marriages are more complex than that. It wasn't just that our embrace left me feeling slightly unnerved, although it did. It was that I had acquired a new picture of my wife—two pictures, in fact. In one of them, she was reading the letter out loud, almost tonelessly, faltering occasionally, and once with a brief tremor in her voice— reading scenes in which she abused her children. In the other picture, she was with our children, with Paul and Fay, in the bath or the shower, doing the things that Dieter Tiberius had described. I didn't believe a word of it, not for a second, and yet those pictures were there and had become a part of my wife. I kept pushing them away, but they came back, just like the pictures I now had in my head of my children and me.

17

THAT AFTERNOON WE HAD AN APPOINTMENT with our lawyer. On the way, we stopped off at kindergarten and impressed on both teachers that on no account were our children to be picked up by a third party, no matter what he said. That is, in any case, a basic rule of our kindergarten: no child may be picked up by anyone who hasn't been authorised by the parents and introduced to the teachers. But we wanted to be on the safe side—we wanted, I think, to feel that there was something we could do. Then we sat hand in hand in our lawyer's office while she read our letters from Dieter Tiberius. For the first time, I was struck by a thought that was to bother me repeatedly in the months to come: What if she believes him rather than us? What if she thinks there's something in his accusations?

Sitting there, I was for the first time a man under the shadow of suspected child abuse, a man faced with the question of how to prove that he hasn't abused his children. I realised that we were now dependent on the trust and goodwill of others. I remember, too, a conscious feeling of uprightness and decency, an almost holy feeling. In the face of the accusations I was the very model of uprightness and decency. And I remember being confident, as I sat in that lawyer's office, that Dieter Tiberius had made a mistake. His perverted letter would enable us to evict him from the house and from our lives—maybe not straight away, but definitely within a few weeks.

'Disgusting,' the lawyer said. 'I'm so sorry you have to be put through this.'

'It's slander,' I said, 'severe defamation.' I had little idea of law and legal terminology at the time—only a sense of justice, of right and wrong. 'It must be easy,' I went on, 'to evict him from his flat on the strength of that.'

The lawyer looked at me and for a while she said nothing. Her dark hair was combed back off her face and secured in a headband, the jacket of her suit hung over her chair, an office classic by Charles and Ray Eames. USM furniture in black, one carefully chosen piece in red, a glass desk, a Dokoupil leopard on the wall, a cork print. Eventually she said something that shattered my confidence: 'Mr Tiefenthaler,' she said, 'unfortunately we live in a state where the law prevails.'

'What do you mean, *unfortunately*?' my wife asked icily.

'I always thought we were fortunate to live in a state where the law prevails,' I added.

The lawyer looked at us somewhat pityingly. 'In your present situation, it is not particularly fortunate,' she said coolly, 'because I fear that your expectation—your reasonable expectation—that this person can be swiftly removed from your vicinity is not easy to fulfil.'

'But presumably we can sue him,' I said naively.

'Of course we can sue him,' the lawyer said—and she would of course set the ball rolling immediately, but that did not mean Tiberius would have to evacuate his flat. She was afraid she could give us no hope in that direction. People were fairly hard to dislodge from their homes in this country, especially when social security was paying the rent, which, given Tiberius's lack of work, seemed likely. She could tell us stories about her own tenants—horrendous. Her contemptuous words made me uncomfortable. I hadn't been thinking of our case in terms of class or social privilege and had no desire to.

My wife said that as she understood it, those who acted lawfully were protected by the law. A long and increasingly trenchant discussion ensued between the two women, but of course got us nowhere. My unease grew. I was a great believer in good behaviour and had this stupid fear that the lawyer might begin to doubt our innocence if we upset her. I intervened, saying that we'd be grateful if she would use all—really *all*—legal means at her disposal. She agreed to that. She took copies of the letters, we signed a power of attorney, and she saw us to the door. If we didn't feel safe, she could organise a gun for us, she said. I shook my head.

In the lift, my wife had one of her fits. I have forgotten what she said, but she screamed all the way down from the fifth floor. When we reached the ground floor, she started to cry. I took her in my arms, but was unable to communicate so much as a spark of optimism. I am a law-abiding citizen—always have been. I believe the law exists so that peaceable people like me can live in peace. Should that peace be disturbed, I believe the law is there to restore it immediately. This trust had been shattered—in a lawyer's office, of all places—but it was only for a few minutes. Back in the car, I, the optimist, my mother's son, was already saying I didn't believe the lawyer.

'The law will protect us,' I said. We drove to a shop that specialised in self-defence and bought my wife a can of pepper spray.

On the windowsill in the common entryway was another letter, a thin one this time. There was only one sheet of paper in the envelope and only a single sentence on the paper: *I forgot to mention in my last letter that I have filed a complaint against you with the police. Dieter Tiberius.*

In the kitchen we discussed what to do next, and eventually decided that my wife would take the children to stay with her mother for a while, down near the Austrian border. While Rebecca collected Paul and Fay from kindergarten, I booked their flights for the following morning. Then, as I was already online, I decided to find out more about our legal situation. I googled terms like 'defamation' and 'stalking', but found nothing to vindicate my optimism. There was no anti-stalking law at that time, and I don't know whether it would have helped us. Dieter Tiberius wasn't exactly a proper stalker, even if we often called him 'our stalker'—and still do.

That afternoon I played with my children. I am a keen Lego builder, which maybe isn't surprising in an architect, but I don't just build houses with Lego—I build cars and ships too. Paul and Fay talked the entire time, as usual, but I barely heard a word of it. My thoughts kept returning to Dieter Tiberius and his attack on our family, and I was tired, too. I hadn't slept for two nights in a row. Once I heard the sound of the toilet being flushed in the basement and felt a rush of hatred.

In the evening, when the children had gone to bed, I walked around the outside of the house, once at nine and once at eleven, nervous and tense, because I knew I might come face to face with Dieter Tiberius at any moment. I kept stopping and listening, and tried to work out how long it would take me to leap to the woodpile next to the garage door—the people who live in the attic flat have a fireplace—and grab myself a cudgel.

After driving my family to the airport the next morning, what I now call the 'active phase' began. History has to be divided up, or else you lose sight of the big picture. I rang the local youth welfare office and asked to be put through to the director. I told him that we had been accused of sexually abusing our children, but that this was not the case, quite definitely not, and he could come around any time he liked to assess our children.

'Who are you?' the director of the youth welfare office asked. I told him our names again and described the situation, once more protesting our innocence.

'It is not pleasant for us, but our children are at your disposal,' I said in a firm voice.

I had read about tests done on children to ascertain whether or not they'd been abused. Among other things, they were made to draw pictures. I don't know what you should or shouldn't draw, but I was sure my children would draw the right things—after all, they hadn't been abused. I couldn't help imagining, though, that they might accidentally draw something wrong—perhaps a tree, which a psychologist might interpret as a phallus—but the very idea was so terrible that I preferred not to think about it.

The director of the youth welfare office said that this was the first time anyone had ever called him to report that they hadn't abused their children. He would look into the matter and get back to me. It was then that it began to dawn on me that we were well on the way to hysteria—but that did nothing to stop us. We justified everything we did by saying that we had to stop Dieter Tiberius from assaulting our children. It was impossible to do too much—only too little. So I was quite satisfied to have made my phone call to the youth welfare office.

Later, I was rung by a youth welfare officer who had called the crime office to investigate and told me that 'the matter' involved allegations 'against unknown individuals'. I didn't understand what that meant—it made no sense. Why unknown? Dieter Tiberius had presumably named us as offenders.

'And what happens now?' I asked.

'Probably nothing for the moment,' the welfare officer said.

I was afraid that some vast secretariat would now deal with us according to its own laws, with neither our knowledge nor our involvement—that we would be crushed in the cogs of a creaking machine. I rang the crime office and was directed with surprising rapidity to the department dealing with so-called 'crimes against the person'. I made an appointment for that afternoon with a Ms Kröger.

Ms Kröger was wearing jeans and a denim jacket and had short, copper-coloured dyed hair. When she gave me her hand, I saw that she had a pistol in a holster under her arm. We sat down. In front of her on the desk was an unopened file. It was slim—almost flat—as if it had very little in it, which could have been reassuring, if it were our file, or alarming, if it were our stalker's. The fatter his file, the more suspect he would be. Behind Ms Kröger hung a poster of two fluffy kittens.

I outlined the situation for her and asserted our innocence. Ms Kröger said that our neighbour hadn't actually done anything, so the police didn't have 'much of a handle' on him. I asked when the police would have a handle.

'If your wife or children were attacked,' she said.

'My wife has been attacked—' I said, 'with words.'

'Physically,' said Ms Kröger.

'Does that mean,' I asked, 'that the police will only intervene when something happens to my wife or children?'

'I can't tell you otherwise,' said Ms Kröger.

'I don't understand,' I said.

She looked at me in silence. A man came in and said, 'We're about to start.'

'I'm coming,' she said and got up.

'Please,' I said, 'just one more minute.'

She sat down again.

'Tell me what we ought to do,' I said.

'Try to obtain a restraining order,' said Ms Kröger.

'What's that?' I wanted to know.

'A court order that requires your neighbour to keep a distance of at least fifty metres from your wife and children,' said Ms Kröger.

'What about the accusation of child abuse?' I asked.

'It's possible your children will have to undergo a psychological evaluation,' she said.

Ms Kröger was by no means forthcoming. In her face I saw no emotion, no inclination to take sides—not even sympathy. I did not have the impression that anyone was being investigated: neither Dieter Tiberius, nor us. The file, unopened throughout, would evidently remain slim, I thought, as I said goodbye.

All the same, I left feeling nowhere near as bad as I might have done. The words 'restraining order' had raised my hopes. If Dieter Tiberius had to keep a distance of at least fifty metres from my wife and children, he wouldn't be able to carry on living in his flat. He would have to move out, and we'd be rid of him.

I rang our lawyer. She was in a meeting and rang back two hours later. She had already considered applying for a restraining order, she said, but she didn't think we'd find a court willing to issue one in our case.

'Why ever not?' I asked, with a hint of desperation in my voice.

'Because he lives in the same building as you, and no court is going to drive him out of his own home,' she said.

'Give it a try, all the same,' I begged.

'All right,' she said.

18

I MADE MYSELF MOZZARELLA and tomatoes for supper, with basil that I cut from a pot in the garden. Then I rang my wife and told her what I'd done that day and how things stood. I admit I glossed over the facts and made the restraining order sound like a real hope, not even mentioning our lawyer's doubts, leaving Rebecca with the impression that things didn't stand too badly at all. I did mention, though, that a performance had begun—a drama in which the truth was not easy to discern. I told her I missed her, which was the truth.

'I miss you too,' she said, and then: 'We're going to make it, aren't we?'

'Yes,' I said. 'You and I, we're going to make it.'

We were a little embarrassed, perhaps because we hadn't spoken to each other so lovingly for a long while. Then I spoke to the children and heard happy reports about a steamboat trip on Lake Constance.

In the evening I watched a football match on television, patrolled the flat and went to bed at half past ten. As I lay there in the dark, I kept looking at the alarm clock; the last time I remember seeing was three o'clock. Until then, at least, I was awake. I wondered why there had to be a threat lurking one storey below me again, just as there had been in my childhood. I don't want to compare my father to Dieter Tiberius, but all the same, I felt a sense of déjà vu.

I wasn't afraid in the way that I had once been afraid of my father, but still I lay in bed with a sense of impending danger. The question troubling me now was that of my own manhood. I was no longer sure that the state was going to help me. It was possible that I would have to take it upon myself to turn Dieter Tiberius out and ensure the safety of my family.

I was assailed by detailed and endlessly spiralling memories of a Christmas Eve we had celebrated a few years ago with our extended family. My parents were there, Rebecca's mother, *her* mother (so my children's great-grandmother) and

Cornelia with her new boyfriend, Mircea. My little brother wasn't there—he only rarely showed up at family gatherings. This time he had rung from Minneapolis-St Paul to make his excuses. He had an assignment that could make a big difference, he told me, and he'd send me an email soon. The email never came.

My sister's marriage had broken up six months before, and for two months now she'd been going out with this new boyfriend, a Romanian from Bucharest who ran a gym in Berlin. That was where my sister had met him. My mother had warned me that Mircea was, as she put it, 'different'. I liked him at first. He was open, warm and extremely good-looking—broad-shouldered and robust. He was a new type for my sister, who had so far spent her life with gentle, not particularly enterprising men. She hadn't wanted children with her husband because she didn't think he was in a position to provide for them, and before he was able to put himself in such a position, she left him. Mircea, on the other hand, was bursting with energy.

Since my wife took charge of our Christmases, they've felt much more festive. While the Christmas trees of my childhood were always meagre affairs, Rebecca organises splendid Nordmann firs that bend even under our high ceilings. My wife has a good eye, so our trees are always tastefully and cheerfully decorated, sometimes in red, sometimes white, sometimes in a golden honey colour. We don't have set Christmas rituals—no one in my family is a devout Christian, except for Cornelia, who flirted with religion at the age of fifteen or sixteen and subsequently embraced it with a vengeance. That was another reason why Mircea came as a surprise to me. The zest for life he exuded was at odds with the image I had of my sister. She did not, however, try to force her beliefs on others, and let us celebrate Christmas as we liked.

First, we all went to church, then presents were opened. This, I am sorry to say, transforms my children year after year into beings completely alien to me. I cannot put it any other way: during that half-hour at the Christmas tree, when Paul and Fay greedily tear open their presents, dashing from one to the next (there's always an enormous heap), and eventually ask a little disappointedly (in spite of the enormous heap) whether that's all—during that half-hour, my children are alien to me. We don't sing carols or recite poems or say prayers, but soon after the presents we have Christmas dinner, which is always cooked by my mother and always the same: stuffed turkey with red cabbage and potatoes, followed by baked apples. My sister said grace. For the rest of us that was always a strange moment, because we didn't know what to do with our hands. On the table? Under the table? Together? One over the other? Where to look? What to think? To begin with, when I was still being a jerk to Cornelia, I think I looked pitying or even scornful. Later

I managed a kind of minute-long trancelike state of inner neutrality—and soon after that she was dead.

I don't know whether we'd have fared better at the Christmas known to the family as the 'Mircea Disaster' if we had had more firmly established rituals. Maybe we'd have kept control of the evening then. Maybe we'd have insisted it went the way we wanted it to—and that our way involved not arguing at Christmas, being considerate of one another, rather than laying into one another. Our idea of Christmas was what you might call a ceasefire.

It didn't get off to a bad start. Mircea was charming to my sister; he was also charming to the other women, including Rebecca's grandmother, always noticing when they needed more gravy or their wine needing topping up. We were all a little bewitched by this kindness and attentiveness, as it was not something we had ever bothered with among ourselves— not on my side of the family, at any rate. Mircea snared us in his never-ending web of stories, a shimmering, silky-soft web. He carried us off to the gargantuan palace that the dictator Ceaușescu had built in Bucharest in the eighties. We roamed with him through staterooms as large as gymnasiums, along endless corridors, into nooks and crannies where no one had ever set foot. We saw magnificent elephantine chandeliers and golden taps, and came across strange, long-forgotten characters doing their duties in remote corners of the palace, laying a mosaic or dusting windowsills.

Mircea himself had worked as an electrician, screwing thousands of light switches into the walls of the palace without an end in sight and without ever meeting another soul. He made it sound as if he were the true master of this giant stone realm, the man who was in control of everything and saw to it that even when there were delays in the delivery of materials, the construction work never flagged. It bothered me that he displayed sympathy for Ceauşescu's dictatorship, but I dismissed it as nostalgic nonsense. After the revolution had swept away Ceauşescu and his wife—I clearly remember the pictures of their corpses—Mircea left for the west, where, after a few false starts, he ended up in Berlin. He then became a fitness trainer and later took over a gym.

At this point in his story—it was after the baked apples—I began to feel uneasy, because Mircea not only knew how to get bodies in shape, he could also heal souls, imagining himself in possession of psychic powers. His hands, the same hands that for years had screwed light switches into the walls of Ceauşescu's palace, were, he believed, miracle-healer's hands. When he caught my sceptical glance, he leapt to his feet and began to massage Rebecca's grandmother's neck. She had complained of aches and pains earlier in the evening. Was it better, he asked after a minute, and what could the old woman say but yes? She was ninety-two. He threw me a look of triumph, and, carrying on with the massage, told us that some bandits, as he called them, had broken into his gym the previous week and stolen his laptop and a stereo.

'And what do the police do?' he asked. From the sneering way he asked, the answer was clear: nothing. 'In Germany the police never do anything,' said Mircea. If he had happened to be walking past his gym that night and seen the burglars, they wouldn't be alive today, that was for sure. It was no good showing mercy to these people—things only got worse and worse—and things were in fact getting worse and worse in Germany. I said we lived in a country where the rule of law prevailed and where the police solved most crimes.

'Ha,' he said, his hands still on Rebecca's grandmother's neck. We were given a long list of thefts and murders left unsolved. The victims were, without exception, acquaintances of his.

I glanced at my father. In the past he had made speeches like this himself, but he had grown meeker in his old age and now voted Green. He was silent, fixing Mircea with a look that seemed more like a prayer—a prayer that this man might turn out to be good for Cornelia, even if it didn't look that way just now.

Germans were simply too soft, said Mircea. All they did was stuff their faces and think about their pensions. They no longer had the guts to defend themselves, and Germany would soon go under.

I got up, went over to the Christmas tree, gouged the burnt-down candles out of their holders and put in new ones.

I made another feeble attempt to defend the rule of law, but Mircea cut me short. His hands had stopped moving and were resting on Rebecca's grandmother's shoulders.

'There are no men here,' he said. 'You have beautiful women,' he added, with a charming glance at my sister and wife, 'but you don't have real men anymore.'

I wondered whether lighting Christmas-tree candles counted as men's work or women's. Fire is associated with cooking—that is why it was more often the women who were in charge of fire back in the Stone Age. So my task couldn't be genuinely masculine—it was feminine, and from a masculine point of view that meant effeminate. On the other hand, I had seen pictures showing men chasing mammoths with torches, so perhaps I was in fact upholding a masculine tradition when I lit the honey-coloured candles with extra-long matches.

'Well, as long as we have beautiful women,' I said, but my pathetic attempt to save the situation with humour fell flat. Mircea went on and on. He railed against 'the overfed Germans' and we made no comment. It was just as he said— we were too soft. But that's only partly true and isn't quite fair.

We already knew at the time that my sister had cancer— breast cancer. Her gynaecologist had diagnosed it two years before, after overlooking it for years. My sister, a conscientious person, had been for regular mammograms, but her doctor had shown himself incompetent. By the time he discovered the breast cancer, it had already spread to the liver—usually a death sentence. But my sister fought with a strength I wouldn't have credited her with. She underwent hormonal therapy, became vegetarian and got up every morning at half past five to do tai chi in the park. The cancer vanished. Cornelia considered herself healthy, a survivor, and we, her family, went along with that, for her sake and for ours. But by then we knew too much about cancer to suppress a particular thought, even if we never voiced it: cancer can hide, it can come back—especially liver metastases. That's why we were glad of anything that did Cornelia good, and a man undoubtedly did her good, especially after the break-up. If she had chosen Mircea because of his putative healing powers, that was fine by me, even if I couldn't believe in them myself. Maybe he was just great in bed. That kind of happiness could ward off cancer too—why shouldn't it? At any rate, we were not going to do anything that got in the way of my sister's happiness. That is another reason we kept silent, another reason I betrayed my values.

It was a double betrayal, because on the one hand I kept silent in the face of this ignorant, brutish view of democracy, civilisation and the rule of law—and on the other hand I sat there wishing my father would go into the spare room, where one of his guns was sure to be lying. My parents always stayed the night with us at Christmas, and we'd had to train my father not to leave his gun under the pillow here, the way he did at home. One of the children might have found it and wreaked havoc. In my anger at Mircea, I imagined my father momentarily holding a gun to his head to stop him talking such bullshit, to show him that we too were capable of defending ourselves. So it was that I was too feeble that Christmas to take a stand for civilisation and at the same time succumbed inwardly to the temptations of barbarism.

The rest of Christmas Eve passed peacefully. In the end Mircea wearied of his tirades and sat down, and was once again charming to everyone. My sister had kept quiet throughout, but now she billed and cooed with her boyfriend as if nothing had happened—as if she had heard nothing to alarm her. I was glad when, long after midnight, the pair of them left.

I thought of Mircea as I lay sleepless in my bed. I wondered what he would have done in my place. There was a good chance Dieter Tiberius would no longer be alive. Or else Mircea would have beaten him up until he moved out. Or tortured him. I wished Mircea was a good brother-in-law so that I could ring him up and get him to take care of things for me. I was ashamed of this wish. I couldn't ring him anyway— not now. He was as dead as my sister—he had died even before she had, in a car crash in Romania. And I wouldn't have rung him, honestly. I believed in the law, just as I believe in it to this day, even if, in our case, a loophole has opened up.

Democracy is often unappealing—too many politicians fooling around—but it is, I think, the best we have, all the same. In a dictatorship the very people who scare me would be in power—the unscrupulous intelligent ones—and to enforce their power they would use the people who scare me even more—the dumb brutal ones. My fear of dictatorship is a fear of subjugation: the unscrupulous intelligent ones telling the dumb brutal ones to beat me up because I like my freedom. Democracy, on the other hand, is a form of government for people who can't or won't resort to physical violence. In the past, you might have said it's a form of government for weaklings. In this traditional sense, I am a weakling—yes, I admit it; I want to assert my position by means of negotiation, not brawls or shootouts. It is very much in our interest as weaklings that it's not dog eat dog. That is why we established the rule of law and set the police to enforce it. Our problem is that we are good at developing a society that protects us, but not good at defending ourselves when it fails us. We don't even like to get into a full-blown fight because we're afraid that cerebral fluid will flow. Nothing makes us as strong or as weak as our brains.

I wondered that night whether I was the man I possibly ought to be just now—I mean a real man, in the classic sense of the word. For the time being my family was unprotected by the state, so all protection had to come from me. Hadn't I failed long ago? Because I hadn't taken Dieter Tiberius on right at the beginning—hadn't acted like an angry gorilla?

I heard the toilet being flushed: Dieter Tiberius was as awake as I was. How humiliating to hear *that* noise from him and have to imagine him wiping the drops from his glans—if he was that fastidious—and then tucking away his penis. And this man desired the same woman I did. That is the trouble with beautiful women: in desiring them you associate yourself with other men, even with idiots, or with sickos like Dieter Tiberius. I fought back this thought, wearily, exhaustedly, and, by a roundabout route, ended up remembering Putu. I saw her dancing: the leopard-skin bikini, the high heels, her firm body. It is the last image I recall from that night.

19

WHEN I GOT UP, the first thing I did was to check in the entryway to see if there was a letter on the windowsill, but there was nothing. I left the house at nine and went to a laundry and drycleaners near the train station. It's not a small business, not somewhere you'd take the odd skirt or shirt, but more like a factory, catering to professional customers: local restaurants or bed and breakfasts. The manager, a man named Thomas Walther, let the basement to Dieter Tiberius.

The woman at the counter sent me to the back of the building through a heavy steel door. I found myself in a kind of small hangar dotted with machinery, including what looked like enormous washing machines. It was hot; damp gathered on my skin. I saw steam and heard a rumbling and a hissing. People in white overalls stood between the machines. Because of the steam I did not immediately recognise Walther. I asked around and found him standing by a machine from which a young woman was pulling white sheets. The two of them were laughing as I approached.

I had thought he would remember me, just as I remembered him from the conversation we'd had with the other homeowners in our building, but he did not. I told him who I was and asked whether I could speak to him in private. The woman was from Moldova and didn't understand a word of German, said Walther. She hadn't let herself be put off by my arrival and carried on pulling sheets from the machine.

His tenant, I said, was seriously harassing my wife—could he, as the man's landlord, not give him notice? It was impossible for us to continue living under the same roof. I was prepared to find a new tenant for the basement and would bear all resulting costs. I had to talk loudly to make myself heard above the rumble and hiss of the machines.

'What's old Dieter been up to then?' asked Walther.

It worried me that he referred to him so familiarly.

'He writes my wife obscene letters,' I said. I could tell from Walther's face that he was not at all perturbed.

'Love letters?' he asked.

'No, obscene letters,' I said. 'About sex, perverted sex.'

He nodded knowingly and then said: 'I've never had any trouble with Dieter.'

'He claims that we are sexually abusing our children,' I said.

The woman from Moldova looked at me. She had pulled all the sheets out of the washing machine and stowed them in a trolley.

'That you're sexually abusing your children,' said Walther, in a semi-questioning tone.

'We don't abuse our children,' I said, and immediately realised that it made me sound guilty as hell. You shouldn't have to tell anyone that you don't abuse your children—it should go without saying. Sweat was pouring down my face. It was hot between the machines, and my shirt and suit trousers were sticking to my skin.

Now Walther looked at me with interest, almost searchingly. 'And what makes Dieter think that?' he asked.

'I don't know,' I said. 'All I know is that I don't want to live a day longer under the same roof as him.'

'He's a good tenant,' Walther said. 'Social security pays the rent, so it's always on time. Have you been to the police? What do they say?' he asked.

'They're still looking into it,' I said.

'Good,' he said, 'let's wait to hear what they have to say, then we can talk again, okay?' His tone wasn't unfriendly, but the conversation had got me nowhere.

'Okay,' I said, despondently, wishing my wife had done the talking. She's better at taking a firm stand than I am—we'd divided up the tasks wrong. On the other hand, I could hardly have left her alone in the house with Dieter Tiberius while I went off to her mother's with the children.

I drove to the office and did some work, without registering what I was doing.

That night I lay awake for a long time again, listening out in the silence and wondering whether Dieter Tiberius was also lying awake in bed, thinking of me the way I was thinking of him. We were at most ten, fifteen metres apart, two men under their bedclothes, their heads on their pillows, apparently tranquil, but horribly embroiled, horribly entwined in each other's lives—one an architect, a married man with a beautiful wife and two children, well-off, middle-class, and the other a former ward of the state, unemployed, alone, on government benefits.

All the advantages were on my side, but I was afraid this might turn out to be a disadvantage, that there were people—social workers, journalists—who would transform this story into a symbolic battle between the poor man in the basement and the wealthy one upstairs. Ultimately it would be my fault, the fault of my class, that Dieter Tiberius had to revolt. People would want to see him win, and me lose, and that desire would propel him to victory. My heart was racing.

The next morning I went to the social welfare office. I had rung up, but was told they didn't provide information over the phone. I enquired at counters, followed directions, made my way through the corridors and sat outside rooms waiting my turn to go in for an excruciatingly long time. Looking at the others waiting too, I saw despondency, grief, indignation and anger, and in the end I got nowhere.

Eventually I found myself in a completely unadorned room, without so much as a potted plant. Two men and a woman sat opposite me at a round table—no file. I told them my story, almost routinely. I told it to blank faces. When I had finished, the woman said they couldn't discuss Dieter Tiberius with me, couldn't even say whether or not social security paid his rent. They would ask me to please accept that, one of the men added.

'I suppose I'll have to,' I said, 'but I'd like to ask you to look at the matter like this: perhaps my neighbour is someone who needs help—and that's a job for the social welfare office, isn't it?' Shrugs, silence. I put down my business card and left.

In the corridor I ran into a man who was so fat that it was impossible to miss him. 'Scuse me,' I mumbled.

'Look where you're going next time,' he called after me.

Fat lump, I thought. Stupid fat lump.

When I got home in the evening I found a letter in my letterbox. It was not from Dieter Tiberius—I saw that at once. The handwriting was different and the envelope was franked. A lawyer informed me that he was representing Dieter Tiberius. That was all the letter said, and yet it sounded threatening to me. I took it to mean that Dieter Tiberius had taken on a lawyer to fight us with all available means. Over dinner, at an Italian place near the station, it occurred to me that the letter might also be a good sign. Tiberius had evidently decided to take the legal route. That was terrain we could prevail on, whatever the cost. The money was there— and if it wasn't enough, I could get hold of more.

I rang my wife and fed her with optimism again. I was, I have to confess, playing the man of action who does all that he can to defend his family—playing the warrior—and I announced my first small successes. In fact, I was getting nowhere. I had heard nothing from the police. My lawyer, I had discovered in a phone call, was unable to organise a restraining order, but this did nothing to rouse the Mircea in me. Even our stalker had gone quiet—until the lawyer's letter arrived, I hadn't seen any sign of him in days. I was beginning to think I was waging a non-existent war.

When I gave my wife a more truthful description of the situation ten days later, she said maybe it really had blown over. 'Maybe he's come to his senses,' she said. We decided that she and the children should return the following day. We'd just have to be careful. My wife said she wasn't afraid of Dieter Tiberius—only afraid for Paul and Fay. I knew exactly what she meant. Nothing makes us as vulnerable—and thus as anxious—as our children.

20

ISN'T IT AWFUL THAT, whether as children or as adults, we can never live without fear? Apart from the fear of my father, the great fear of my youth was nuclear war. You didn't have to know much about the arms race, didn't have to understand anything—a single sentence was enough to send shivers down your spine. *After a nuclear attack everything is destroyed and everybody is dead.* I only had to look out of the window of the bus and tell myself that none of these houses would be left standing, only had to look around my class and tell myself that none of these children would be left alive, and the terror set in. Nuclear war was an abrupt change from a life of promise to nothingness, and nobody had a chance. The thoughts I could usually rely on to ward off fear failed me here. When I was seized with panic that the plane I was in was going to crash, I would tell myself that one person was going to survive and that person would be me. Such cases existed, I knew they did. But in a nuclear war nobody escaped alive and it wasn't even desirable to be spared. What could I possibly do all alone in a radioactive wasteland? Rats as big as dogs. I wasn't yet familiar with the word 'mutant', but I knew, though no one had ever told me, that nuclear rays could somehow turn ordinary creatures into monsters. Then there was cancer. The fear of nuclear warfare was the fear of death *and* the fear of life. That was what made it so insidious. I often lay awake long into the night imagining the world's disappearance—and with it my own.

That's how I became a pacifist, if my father's guns hadn't already made one of me. When I was sixteen or seventeen I began to read books and articles on disarmament like a man possessed. I soon knew all the acronyms and watchwords of that strange era: SALT I, MIRV, flexible response, equilibrium of terror, SALT II, SS-20, Pershing II, zero option. I stuck a dove of peace, white on a blue background, on my bedroom door—on the outside, so that my father could see it. It was ages since he'd last set foot in my room.

When my music (reggae, at the time) was too loud for him, he would yell up the stairs at me, and when the music was so loud I couldn't hear him, he would fling open the door to my room and yell again, but he didn't come in.

When in October 1981 the peace movement called for a demonstration in Bonn, the West German capital, I went along with a few friends. We were protesting NATO's 'double-track decision', instigated in large part by the West German chancellor, Helmut Schmidt, who feared that a growing imbalance between the Warsaw Pact countries and NATO left us vulnerable. Schmidt's argument was that we had to force the Soviets to agree to limit the kinds of weapons that could be deployed—and that the only way we could do so was to develop similar weapons ourselves first. We saw this as madness.

It was shortly before our leaving exams but, seeing that the survival of the human race was at stake, we had asked to be let off lessons. The teachers were divided: those who, like us, were against NATO's counter-armament wanted to let us off; the others, who supported Helmut Schmidt, were against it. The headmaster ruled that we should attend lessons on the day of the demonstration, but a teacher who was on our side said no one was going to punish our absence, and so it was decided.

We took the train. The East German border guards who inspected our identity cards were friendlier than ever before:

no searches, no nastiness. For the first time, I saw those grey-uniformed men and women smile, and when they left, silence fell on our compartment. We had read in the conservative press that we were the fifth column of the Eastern bloc, that we were helping Brezhnev towards world domination. We laughed—we had no sympathy with real-life socialism. We had been to East Berlin too often to find life there acceptable. We wanted peace, wanted to save the world, and believed that every additional rocket made nuclear war more likely. And now we had been treated like Warsaw Pact allies. For a few kilometres we felt bad, but we shook it off, opened a bottle of Martini and held a celebration, though only a modest one. Things were too serious for us to get drunk. We arrived in Bonn at night, hung around the station for a while and later grew cold on benches by the Rhine.

The next day I stood in the vast crowd in the Hofgarten, listening to speeches in favour of peace and disarmament, and thinking of my father. I hadn't talked to him for ages. Provocation was now my only mode of interaction with him, and when he wasn't getting worked up about things I'd said, he ignored me. I don't want to claim that relations between us were like those between the US and the Soviet Union, because neither my father nor I was thinking in terms of annihilation. There was no equilibrium of terror, either, but only, to use another term common at that time, a tense coexistence. I resolved to take home something of the desire for peace I had seen there in the Hofgarten.

First I spoke to my mother, knowing that my father's guns were a cause of suffering to her, too. Her war had been more difficult than his, and she wanted nothing to do with guns. That she chose this man and has remained with him to this day is one of love's miracles. She agreed to my plan, as expected, and so one afternoon when my father was at the car dealership, she and I drew up a disarmament treaty together with my sister and brother. I had read and heard such a lot about it already that I knew just what to do, and I talked of confidence-building measures and aides-mémoire, ranting on and on until my little brother started to grumble that he didn't understand a word of it. At any rate, I said, we wouldn't get anywhere unless we made our father some kind of offer.

'You,' I said to my little brother, 'could stop smoking.'

'But he doesn't smoke,' said my mother.

'Of course he smokes,' I said.

'Do not,' said my little brother.

My mother got terribly upset, because she believed me rather than my little brother, and rightly so, and in the end my brother agreed to stop smoking. We did, however, have to promise we wouldn't tell Dad that he ever had smoked.

'Otherwise he'll be firing one last shot before he scraps his guns,' my little brother said.

'Your father doesn't shoot at his children,' said my mother, and the topic of smoking was dropped from the negotiations.

It was even harder with my sister. In my parents' eyes, she essentially did nothing wrong.

'Cornelia could take up shooting again,' said my little brother. She had stopped when she turned eighteen. We had all noticed my father's disappointment, but he had accepted it uncomplainingly.

'We can't open disarmament negotiations with someone announcing she's going to take up shooting,' I said. 'That goes against the spirit of the talks. They're supposed to make the world safer, not unsafer.'

'I don't make the world unsafe when I shoot,' said my sister. 'I only shoot at targets, and unlike you, I actually hit them.'

That was aimed at me, and usually I'd have said something even nastier back to her, but I was serious about preparing for our upcoming talks, and although it wasn't easy, I restrained myself.

'How about *you* give up being so arrogant?' my sister said. 'Dad would be sure to hand over all his guns then.'

Now I'd really had enough.

'Not even God could cure you of your stupidity,' I sneered.

Our mother intervened. Peacemaking was, I think, the role she was most often called upon to perform. She was good at it, and in the end we had got together a pretty good catalogue of offers for my father. Tidying up was one of them, not leaving bikes in front of the garage door, having shorter showers, mowing the lawn, using headphones when we listened to music. My mother agreed to take extra driving lessons, so that our cars didn't always get scratches and dents when she parked them.

'And what are we going to demand?' I asked.

'That he sells all his guns,' said my little brother.

'A zero option then,' I said.

'You think you're so smart,' said my sister.

'Maybe we'll start with half,' my mother said, and we agreed on that.

I suggested that I conduct negotiations with my father during a walk in the woods. I remembered the cheerful, high-spirited mood of those walks with my father, as he planned journeys of adventure for the two of us. The others objected: they wanted to be present. My sister probably thought her personal contributions to the family's peace would snowball if she didn't keep an eye on me. We agreed instead to have a special dinner.

It went badly. I had prepared a long speech full of references to the global situation, but it left my father cold. When he realised what we were driving at, he said only one word: 'Never.' We tried to insist, keeping the tone friendly, but he only ate his turkey leg in silence, a black look on his face, until suddenly he threw down his knife and fork, leapt up and stormed out. He hasn't sold a single gun to this day—not that he can use his guns now anyway, of course, because the police have seized them all.

I spent just under a year still living at home after this disaster, until I'd finished my leaving exams. Then I went away to university, and my father and I practically stopped speaking.

I have often thought about my teenage years since then, weighing the good against the bad, but never coming to a clear-cut conclusion. Of course there were upsides: friends, my first girlfriends. I had a way with people, and I was a good student, too, well liked and well respected. But all that is overshadowed by those anxious hours when I thought my little brother or I might be shot. I had a happy childhood, but not a happy youth. What was worse, I lacked a father— he was reserved, even disdainful. But I have a theory that unhappiness early in life is later transformed into happiness. I always wanted to get away—away from those guns, away from my father—and as a result I had goals. I was ambitious and still am. That helped me to become a successful architect. This theory reconciles me, in part at least, to my youth, but at the same time it worries me. What about my children, who have parents who do everything they can to make them happy? Can happiness early in life also be translated into happiness later on? I don't know.

Memories are slippery at the best of times. Not long ago, I bumped into an old schoolfriend in a Munich hotel, a friend

I had lost touch with. Meeting Saif I met my younger self, but that self turned out to be one I didn't recognise. For a long time, I have thought of my story—the story I tell myself and others about who I am—as one of nonviolence, but Saif made me question it. We talked a lot about the past, of course, and at some point he asked me whether I knew what had shocked him about me. I didn't. He said I had once had a fight with Schiephake outside our classroom— did I remember Schiephake? I only vaguely remembered Schiephake. I had forgotten his first name, and Saif had too.

'You won the fight,' said Saif, 'and he was lying underneath you, and you took his head and banged it several times against the floor.'

'No, I can't believe that,' I said.

'That's how it was,' said Saif.

I have no reason to doubt him, but two things alarm me: that I did it, and that I forgot about it. If you can forget something like that, something that would drastically change how you see yourself, how can you ever know who you truly are?

So what is my story? Maybe, in one of his fits of rage, my father really did hold a revolver to my head and threaten to pull the trigger. Since Saif's revelation, I tell this story tentatively. There is always something new we can learn.

A greater source of worry to me lately is the fact that you can have memories of things that didn't happen. For instance,

I sometimes worry that our children might one day come up with the idea that they were sexually abused by me or my wife. After all, the suspicion was voiced, even if it was voiced by the dubious Dieter Tiberius. It is a part of our family's story. Paul or Fay might unconsciously have picked up on it, and, at some point in the future, if things are going badly for them, they might imagine that they were once abused.

21

WHEN MY WIFE RETURNED from her mother's place with the children, it was twenty hours before she found another letter on the windowsill in the entryway. She rang me in the office and told me Dieter Tiberius was claiming he'd sent emails to RTL, Sat. 1 and the *Bild*. We knew what they were interested in, he said. My wife went down to the basement with the letter in her hand and 'confronted' him, as she put it, probably vociferously. He had only grinned impertinently.

I took the letter to our lawyer and a photocopy to Ms

Kröger at the crime office. They both said it wouldn't make much difference, but for me it made a huge difference. This was the beginning of what I call, in retrospect, the surveillance phase. When I turned into our street in the evening, I expected to see a row of vans with logos on their sides, and reporters with microphones and camera crews. No such vehicles appeared, but there was a camera with me all the time: my own camera, the one in my head. I began to see my life through a camera lens. It was the life of a man who was not a child abuser.

When I went to the playground with Paul and Fay, I behaved like a man who did not abuse his children. I had no idea how to go about it, so I just behaved as I normally would, except that I now did it with a kind of conscious solemnity, aware at all times that I was being normal, that I did not abuse my children. I saw myself through the eyes of policemen, detectives, journalists, social workers and whoever else was part of the infernal cast of my waking dreams. Trying to withstand their stern gaze, I was law-abiding to the point of fastidiousness, never so much as dropping a gum wrapper on the ground. I'd never littered in the past either, but now I did it as a man who did not abuse his children.

Thus my day-to-day life, my normality, became a performance. I acted out harmlessness, I acted out not-being-a-child-abuser. But this conscious not-being is also a form of being, so that consciously not-being-a-child-abuser is a form of being-a-child-abuser. That's my logic. It's the way it felt to me. In the process of affirming what I wasn't, images popped up in my head that had never been there before. I saw things I did not do to my children, never had done, never would do. I was no longer myself: I was my own negative, my own opposite. Until then I had fought Dieter Tiberius, if you can call it fighting, as a stranger: the man downstairs, the madman in the basement, and, in moments of anger, the bastard. That was over now. He had wormed his way inside me. I was fighting myself, fighting the thoughts and images that haunted me. I didn't even tell my wife, I was so ashamed.

It has taken me a great deal of time and effort to feel that I belong to the middle class. There is nothing middle class about guns, and I grew up in a house full of them. Shooting as a sport is of course traditionally associated with the aristocracy, but at the other end of the social scale the possession of a weapon often denotes involvement in criminal activity. The stolidly middle-class German *Bürger* sets too much store by his good name to get mixed up in anything so dubious. Our reputation is an all-enveloping cloak, but it can soon fall into tatters. This is why the bourgeoisie are so anxious: we rely upon the good faith of others. It is not enough to be upright and decent—you must be *seen* to be upright and decent. A rumour, even an unfounded one, can be enough to destroy you.

I saw myself as a headline in the newspapers I don't read,

the newspapers that shout at me from the station kiosk with their violent headlines, telling me things I don't want to know. *Is Star Architect a Child Abuser?* One such question is all it takes. It practically answers itself. You're done for. I'm not a star architect—far from it. I have my strengths and a certain standing, but I am not Calatrava or Herzog. I am not Kollhoff. The headline writers, however, like to use the word 'star' to arouse interest. If I read a headline at the station kiosk telling me that a football star has hit his trainer, I know the culprit plays in the second league. If it were Bastian Schweinsteiger, the headline would read: *Schweinsteiger Hits Trainer.* A star is called by his name; a non-star is a star. That's the way it works. I would be a star architect, and as a result fall even lower in the eyes of the readers. From star to child abuser, ah ha, very bad.

'You and your middle-class values,' my brother sometimes says with a laugh. He was there when I happened to say at one of our soirees that I considered it a duty of the middle class to vote.

'What do you mean by *middle class?*' a woman asked, a journalist, and her tone was so sharp that I knew at once what she was driving at: that I wasn't middle class.

There were nine of us that evening: the journalist and her husband, who is an investment banker; a theatre director and his partner, who calls himself a gallerist but has no gallery at present; a specialist in lung diseases and his new girlfriend, who's in PR, mainly at the ministry for family affairs—and my little brother, partnerless as usual. We'd had a good evening until then. We ate wild boar ragout because my father had shot a wild boar and brought us a shank and a piece of saddle, and we drank the excellent Black Print, a cuvee so dark that it stains your gums blue. I started off the main course with a little anecdote about my father, saying that there had been sides of wild boar, haunches of venison and hares hanging in the garage at home—a source of distress to my sister, who felt sorry for the animals. She never touched the meat, to the delight of my brother and me—all the more for us to dig into.

The lung specialist's new girlfriend, whom we had never met before, was immediately curious about my father when she heard this. I told her about the guns and a bit about what my father was like; my little brother chipped in every now and then, and the PR woman kept staring at the tattoo on his neck. It is the shimmering blue face of some sinister creature; my brother, who designed it himself, says that it's Klingsor. We talked for some time. My father always makes for a good story and everyone listened spellbound. Guns are no longer part of a normal life these days, and what is more interesting than hearing about aberrations?

When we had finished, the gallerist-without-a-gallery pointed out that I had said 'at home' when I was talking about my parents' house.

'Really?' I asked, rather incredulously, but the investment banker had also heard it, and my brother said with a grin: 'Those were your words.'

'This is my home,' I said, glancing at Rebecca, and soon everyone at the table was deep in discussion about when you stopped saying 'home' to refer to your parents' house. The journalist said never: she still said she was going home when she went to her parents' in Regensburg. The specialist in lung diseases said when you had children. My wife said when you stopped going to your parents' for Christmas and had them round to yours.

I opened the sixth bottle of Black Print, although there was still half a bottle on the table and another open bottle waiting. It is essential to give Black Print time to breathe, and over the years I have developed a good feeling for the pace of a dinner party. This one was medium-fast: two hearty drinkers, one sipper and everyone else doing brisk justice to the wine. Most people underestimate the punch of that 14.5 per cent.

Then talk turned to politics, and that was when I spoke the words that provoked the journalist's sharp reaction. Now I had to provide a definition of 'middle class', but that wasn't a problem. It was a subject I had given a great deal of thought.

'The desire for education is definitely part of it,' I said, 'and that includes working on your own education. Keeping your cool is also important,' I continued. 'The middle classes don't get excited or hysterical.'

Money was part of it, but didn't dominate everything. People who were genuinely middle class considered it unreasonable to live their lives at the mercy of figures—share prices, dividends, interest rates. Family was essential—but by family, I said, I meant any kind of permanent ties. On the one hand a respectable lifestyle, but at the same time a few secrets—or least the possibility of them—which must be scrupulously guarded. The middle classes also showed an interest in what was going on in the world, especially politics, because they knew it was politics that shaped the course of their lives. And a sensitivity to questions of freedom— that was my final point, deliberately kept until last and pronounced casually but emphatically.

As soon as I had finished, silence fell on the dining room. I took a gulp of Black Print. My little brother, who had looked at me attentively but somewhat pityingly throughout, raised his glass in a mock toast.

Now the journalist said, 'For me, being middle class is mainly to do with tradition.' I knew that her father had taken over a small clothes shop from his father and enlarged it into a medium-sized clothes shop. What was I to say? The journalist's definition excluded me, and after hearing my story about our father, she knew it. I was too wounded to give a quick-witted response.

'Doesn't that sound rather feudal?' said my wife, rushing to my help. 'Aren't middle-class values acquired and aristocratic ones inherited?' This grabbed the interest of everyone at table except the PR woman, who was engrossed in reading and writing texts on her phone. They debated the question at some length, but I was too annoyed to follow the discussion properly.

The last of the guests left at two; they had all thanked us for an enjoyable evening.

'Why can't you just drop it?' my little brother asked when we were sitting in the kitchen, rather light-headed, less from the wine than from the scent of the flowers our guests had brought my wife, which were spread out among four vases on the kitchen table. 'You know what it was like at Mum and Dad's,' said my little brother.

'But we've all moved on,' I said, 'or at least I have.'

'It's not that easy,' he said. 'How old will you be before you realise that there's no escaping your roots?' He was grinning. My little brother can grin in a terribly demonic way. This isn't so much to do with his face, which is friendly and perpetually boyish; it comes about in the interplay with that sinister figure on his neck, who seems to take up my brother's grin and yoke it to his own.

I looked at my little brother. The mood was just right for a fight. He called me pretentious, conformist, cynical, uptight, pathetic. I called him irresponsible, fake, childish, freeloading, crazy. This was jealousy, of course—I envied my brother's freedom and spontaneity, and he wished, at least some of the time, that he was settled and stable like me—but the real nastiness began when we started accusing each other of treating our parents badly.

I said: 'You exploit them.'

He said: 'You could make it up with Dad.'

We had always fought like this: it was a way of clearing the air, venting our anger and frustration. Afterwards, we would say how lucky we were to have each other, and that neither of us knew what we'd do if we didn't. This time, however, my wife intervened, coming to take me off to bed. Hugs all round. My wife and my brother. My brother and I. 'Mate,' he said.

Rebecca and I weren't having sex at that time. Dieter Tiberius in his basement had cramped our style, I suppose. On one of my patrols I had found a ladder in the bushes beneath our bedroom window. So he had been watching us. He had seen me losing myself, seen my wife's nakedness, the lovely, elegant way she came; maybe he had even heard the vulgar things I said. He had seen us having sex, and the disgust he aroused in us contaminated the act, our desire poisoned by his greedy looks.

Other than that, we were getting along well, drawn together by the threat we faced. I no longer avoided Rebecca: we held one another, consoled one another, talked about our common purpose, about the fight we had on our hands. Our marriage seemed whole again. We simply absorbed Dieter Tiberius into our Anyway World. Apart from that, nothing changed. But then something happened that still distresses me when I think of it.

One evening, maybe three or four weeks after Rebecca's return from her mother's, I found myself—I can't put it any other way—back in Luna. Dieter Tiberius had been quiet for a while, and we had started wondering if he might have given up, if we no longer had reason to be afraid of him. Our fight was not over: as long as we were living under the same roof, Dieter Tiberius remained a threat to Rebecca and the children. All the same, I went to Luna that evening.

I don't think I thought about it at all: it was as if I were on autopilot, and then there I was, in a kind of reverie, sketching drafts, eating my way through six courses. It was only between courses four and five, between ox cheeks braised in brown ale with chestnuts and chicory, and Mont d'Or fondue with walnut bread, pear and celery, that it occurred to me that I was exposing my wife and children to danger, but I took solace in the thought that Dieter Tiberius was hardly going to attack my family in our flat.

I tore a sheet off my roll of drafting paper, always an ugly noise; it makes the people at the nearby tables interrupt their tete-a-tetes to look round at me—the man sitting so strangely alone in front of his semolina flambé with date and

173

ginger marmalade and brown butter ice-cream. It was more embarrassing to me than usual, and it suddenly occurred to me to wonder if I weren't perhaps hoping that Dieter Tiberius would put an end to my marital troubles for me.

I laid down my spoon; I had gone off the date and ginger marmalade. I reassured myself that you sometimes think preposterous things for which there is no basis, but I didn't know if this was a scientifically proven fact or merely a convenient theory I had come up with in a desperate attempt to convince myself. I pushed the thought aside, but didn't finish my dessert or order a digestif or an espresso. I drove home, my heart pounding.

Dieter Tiberius was watching television; that reassured me, because I didn't consider him cold-blooded enough to sit and watch a film after committing a triple murder. My children lay breathing in bed, and my wife was gently snoring, no blood anywhere. I cleaned my teeth and swore never to abandon my family again.

22

IN THE DAYS THAT FOLLOWED I went back to the crime office and to the lawyer. Nothing happened; we were getting nowhere. On 2 June, my wife rang me in the office, her voice even higher than usual. Our daughter had invited her friend Olga round to play. They had played together for a while and then Rebecca had been going to take them for a drive in the country. As she was leaving the house, Dieter Tiberius came out from the basement and told my wife that he had heard her sexually abusing Fay and Olga. She must stay right where she was; the police would be there any minute.

'You are a child abuser,' he said to Rebecca. Those were his very words. She was still screaming and shouting at him when the police car drew up—Sergeant Leidinger and his colleague. Dieter Tiberius reported Rebecca to the police while she and the girls stood there beside them. If someone calls the police and voices suspicions of child abuse, the police have to come and take a report, whether or not they believe the allegations. Afterwards, the two policemen drove off. My wife had gone back into our flat and called me.

'I'll be right with you,' I said, and took a taxi home.

When I got there I stormed straight down to the basement flat, rang the bell, pounded on the door and did a lot of shouting. I don't know exactly what I shouted; I was so upset that I have forgotten the precise words. Something about beating Dieter Tiberius up, but also that he was sick and needed help. I certainly didn't shout that I'd kill him, which is what he claimed to the police when he reported me.

The same police who had responded to his report of child abuse came to our flat an hour later and confronted me with Dieter Tiberius's assertion that I had threatened him with murder. I have no memory of it; I denied it at the time and I stick to that. The policemen were friendly and I gathered from the looks they gave that they were on our side, not Dieter Tiberius's. I asked them what I ought to do next, and they shrugged.

'What would you do?' I asked.

Sergeant Leidinger shrugged again; the other man grinned and put a hand to the holster on his hip. Maybe it was a chance gesture, but at the time I took it to mean that he would settle the matter with his gun.

My dismay knew no bounds. If a policeman believed the only solution was to take matters into our own hands, we could hope for nothing from the law. When I confided this to Rebecca after the policemen had left, she agreed.

As soon as my son got back from visiting a friend, we sat down with the children at the kitchen table and explained to them what Dieter Tiberius accused their parents of having done. We had no choice, now that Fay had heard her mother being called a child abuser. We hadn't even taught our daughter the facts of life, so I had to go back a long way, but soon noticed from Fay's giggles that she already had a vague idea of what sex was about.

I cleared my throat. 'Dieter Tiberius,' I said, 'claims that Mama and Dada do those things to you.'

Of all the sentences I have uttered in my life, that was the most awful. Fay looked at me in bewilderment. Paul grinned.

'That's not true,' said Fay.

'No,' said Paul.

Although I knew those were the only answers they could give, I was relieved.

'Why does he say that?' asked Paul.

'He's a horrid person,' said my wife. 'We haven't done anything to him, but he's horrid to us.'

We tried to reassure them, saying that he couldn't do anything to us—that we would be very careful, and they were quite safe.

'Otherwise Uncle Bruno will come,' said Paul, 'and then he'll be sorry.'

'Yes,' I said, 'Uncle Bruno will beat him up good and proper if he tries anything else.' The children laughed and clapped. 'And so will I,' I said.

Rebecca laid a hand on my arm and gave me a supportive smile. She knew what I was wondering. Why did the children depend on my little brother to protect them rather than their father? It made sense, of course: when Bruno came to see us, he charged around the flat and garden with them for hours on end; he was wild, he had that tattoo on his neck and he could tell them stories of his adventures in South America and Africa. They loved and admired him. Of course they loved me too, no doubt about it, but they knew me as a gentle father who built with them and played with them, but was in no way wild. For that, they had Uncle Bruno. I had always been fine with that, but now it pained me.

After we had put the children to bed, my wife and I sat at the kitchen table again and discussed what we should do. We no longer pinned any hopes on the authorities; there would be no rescue from that quarter.

'*Should* we move?' I asked. We had discussed that particular solution once before, but rejected it. It was so obvious—a clean break, ridding ourselves of the monster by leaving it behind. But we had agreed that we didn't want to be driven away; we were in the right and had no intention of yielding to wrong. We loved our flat: it was our home, our middle-class stronghold, provision for our old age. We'd had that conversation two weeks ago. Now we were more desperate. I would have left, but my wife still refused.

'No way,' she said. 'If anyone here leaves, it's our Untermensch.' She got up and left the room, and a moment later I heard her brushing her teeth.

I was a little startled at Rebecca's choice of words, though I don't think she meant it in any Nazi sense. She wasn't imputing inferiority to Dieter Tiberius; she meant it architecturally, topographically. The fact that she said he was *our* Untermensch underscores this meaning: she was specifically referring to him living under us, in the flat below.

In the next two weeks nothing happened. We lived our Anyway Life and, one evening, in spite of my vow, I went to Beluga, the only starred restaurant in town I hadn't yet tried. I was eating tataki of young venison on oak-wood charcoal with quince, ginger and liquorice, and talking to the sommelier about the wine, which I thought too overpowering for the tender young venison, when he suddenly gave me a funny look, shocked and slightly disgusted. At the same moment, I felt a tickle beneath my left nostril.

'Your nose is bleeding,' said the waiter.

I dabbed the skin above my lip with my left index finger and felt a thick fluid. I held the finger up to my eyes and saw blood, my blood. The sommelier, once again the embodiment of charm and composure, handed me a starched napkin.

'Are you unwell?' he asked.

'No, no,' I said hurriedly. My nose didn't bleed heavily, but it bled for a long time, gradually staining the napkin red. In somebody's company it would have been embarrassing enough, but alone it was unbearable. In top restaurants, the single man is eyed with mistrust as it is. He is suspected of eavesdropping on the tables next to him; he is thought too odd to have a wife or friend; he is despised for the nerve-grating rip of his drafting paper. With a nosebleed, however, he is the sick man, the leper, ruining everyone else's festive evening, their five-hundred-euro evening, by imposing his loneliness on them and then not even managing to cope with it, but bleeding all over the place in rather a pathetic way.

I cut short the dinner after I had staunched the bleeding, paid for the entire meal and drove home. My wife was sitting curled up on the sofa above Dieter Tiberius's flat, reading a novel. I stopped in the doorway and, pointing to the floor, I said, 'He's not the one destroying my family—it's me.'

23

I MET REBECCA in the university canteen when we were both studying in Bochum. I had moved there after leaving school, wanting to get away from my parents, but also away from Berlin, my parents' town. I had known for a long time that I wanted to study architecture; it was an obvious choice for me because I liked drawing. The downside of leaving was that in Berlin, unlike Bochum, I would have been exempt from national service. But I didn't care.

I took a one-bedroom flat, studied architecture, worked

on a construction site on the side and waited for my draft notice, which did indeed come a few months later. I had a medical and applied to be exempted from military service as a conscientious objector. My hearing was classic: a few old men, one of them a war invalid with only one arm. They asked this and that and eventually came to the crux of the matter: 'You're walking in the woods with your girlfriend. All of a sudden you come face to face with three Russian soldiers who want to rape her. You can prevent it, because you have a gun. What do you do?'

My generation was prepared for this question. There were ways of arguing that allowed you to keep the Russians in check or even shoot them and still pretty much pass for a pacifist. I knew the tricks; there were books, there were briefings. But I had decided on a different approach. I said I wouldn't shoot under any circumstances, that it was impossible for me to attack a human being. I would try to dissuade the three men by talking to them.

'But they refuse to be dissuaded,' said the man who only had one arm.

'I wouldn't shoot,' I said.

'Then your girlfriend gets raped—is that what you want?' asked another of the old men.

'Of course not,' I said, 'but I can't shoot. It's impossible for me.'

'Then your girlfriend gets raped,' said the one-armed man.

'I can't shoot at humans,' I said.

Things went back and forth like this for a while. Then the men sent me out while they consulted. I passed the test. The chairman of the committee said they were sure I would end up shooting, but I had nevertheless defended my standpoint with such determination that there was no denying my pacifist convictions. I was exempted from military service and permitted to serve in the community instead. But first I put in a few semesters at the university.

To begin with it was the usual student life of those days: idling, drinking beer, playing cards, a few friends— sometimes a girlfriend, but never for long. At Christmas I went back to my parents' place, where nothing had changed. My sister was studying fashion design at art school, and was still living at home, just like my little brother, who was at school. We had one of our puny Christmas trees, ate turkey, played Scrabble with my mother while my father read, and got on peaceably enough.

When I was in my fourth semester, my little brother turned up on my doorstep and said, 'I've come to live with you.' I didn't want that—I didn't want him to drop out of school—but I couldn't send him away. He got the room that had been my sitting room until then. We worked together on the construction site, went drinking together, argued and fought, and I gave advice to the girls he made unhappy. Sometimes I slept with them, but only after they had asked my little brother if it was all right. At first I enjoyed living together, but then my little brother was out a lot, I didn't know where, and when I saw him in the morning, I knew he'd been partying too hard. Later he told me he'd done 'everything except shooting up' at that time.

Some nights he was so wasted that I would read to him for hours, afraid that he'd never wake up again if he fell asleep. I read *The Lord of the Rings*, which in those days, before the films, was a book for people who thought they were different. I read to fight my brother's glassy eyes, to stop him from drifting off. Sometimes I shouted the words out to keep him awake, and when his drooping eyelids hadn't come up for a while, I would hit him. It was at that time that my brother began to draw pictures, pen-and-ink pictures with motifs from *The Lord of the Rings*. They were to form the basis of his later career and I am a little proud to have given him that start.

After a year and a half, my brother disappeared. I had begun my national service in the old people's home and came back to the flat one evening to find a note on the kitchen table, saying: *Thanks, big bro*. I went straight to his room and saw that his things weren't hanging there anymore. I rang around, but nobody knew where my little brother had gone. My mother and sister didn't know either. We worried about him, and it wasn't until six months later that I got a postcard from Montevideo, half in pictures, half in words.

If I understood correctly, Bruno had joined the navy and was travelling halfway around the world on the destroyer *Mölders*.

'Can you make anything of it?' I asked my mother.

'He's his father's son,' she said.

'And me, who am I then?' I asked.

'You too,' she said.

A few weeks after resuming my studies, I met Rebecca in the canteen. I was sitting alone at a table, eating chicken fricassee smothered in ketchup, when she joined me and said, 'You're someone I'd like to get to know.' I was so surprised, I couldn't think of anything to say. 'Can you talk?' she asked.

'Yes,' I said.

I had seen her around quite a bit. She had mid-length black hair and a dark complexion, and she was slightly plump—not fat, but agreeably plump. In the middle of her forehead she had a mole, almost exactly in the middle, which bothered me at first, because I don't think striking features belong in the middle; they should be off-centre, at least from a graphic point of view. She was a Mediterranean type, but spoke without an accent.

'Are you sure?' she asked. 'Or do you need some help?'

'I'm all right,' I said, and told her my name and my major.

'And why architecture?' she asked.

If I remember correctly, I gave her an extremely long answer. 'Look at the kinds of cities we live in,' I said. 'Look

185

at the houses. Look at the world.' It wasn't, I told her, enough to want to build houses or cities. You had to build worlds. That's what I was like at the time. I had big plans and thought megalomania was a good characteristic, not a bad one. I conjured up worlds before Rebecca's eyes, worlds I wanted to build, worlds where living and working and shopping and everything else would come together in a new way—and I didn't just say that to impress Rebecca. I really meant it. I took out a pad of paper and made sketches, which I explained to her in detail, and now and then I looked up and saw that Rebecca was looking not at the sketches of the new worlds, but at me.

Rebecca and I often went out together after that, drinking and dancing, and we saw plays at Bochum's playhouse, but it was a while before it was love. Rebecca was studying medicine. Her father is a classicist at the university in Aix-en-Chapelle; her mother is a dermatologist, who has black hair like Rebecca, although she isn't from the Mediterranean; she's from the German-speaking minority of Belgium. Because of that I later called Rebecca 'my Spanish Dutch girl' sometimes, although she didn't much like it. Nobody knows where the dark colouring in her family comes from.

Sometimes she would start the day by saying today we had to address each other formally and we would call each other 'Herr' and 'Frau' until the evening. Or she would say today we were characters in a Chekhov play and she would address me as Ivan Ivanovich and I would call her Anna Petrovna, and she would say things like: 'Character, Ivan Ivanovich, you're always harping on about character,' and I would say things like: 'Don't you agree that it's boring, Anna Petrovna, deathly boring?' They weren't quotations; we didn't know the plays that well. We only acted out the spirit of the thing.

It was six months before Rebecca moved in with me. We hadn't yet slept with one another at that point, but there followed amazing years with one another: sex until we wanted no more, until we couldn't anymore, but kept on all the same because we had to. Nothing was to come to an end, no conversation, no outing, no journey, and if anything looked as if it might come to an end because some duty called, we would back out of the duty, and when that was no longer possible because it would have meant living without a degree, without friends, without fillings in our teeth, we parted with a pain usually reserved for the emigrant docks.

'Those years are our seminal myth,' Rebecca once said to me later. 'When I can't get through to you, and I don't mean on the phone—I mean when I can't get through to you even when you're in the flat, even when you're sitting right next to me—then I think of our seminal years and I think to myself that what we had then can't have disappeared, that it will come again.' I like this notion, although I have sometimes wondered whether that seminal myth didn't lull us into a false sense of security, whether it wasn't one reason we accepted my descent into lovelessness.

After three years, my little brother came back. He rang the doorbell and told me over the intercom that I had to come down.

'Don't you want to come up?' I asked.

'No, I have to show you something,' he said.

I ran down, curious to know why he would insist on being reunited on the street after all this time. The first thing I noticed was the tattoo on his neck, then the long hair. We hugged, and I saw a motorbike parked on the pavement, a chopper with a long front fork and a low saddle. Tank, mudguard and side panels were elaborately decorated and I understood at once that Bruno had painted them; it was his style, his way of creating worlds—sombre, mystical worlds that owed much to *The Lord of the Rings*.

'So what do you think?' he asked after we had hugged, glancing at the bike.

'Very nice,' I said.

'A bit more enthusiasm, please,' he said. 'How about magnificent, ravishing, breathtaking?' He boxed me in the chest, I boxed back and we were in each other's arms again.

'Where did you get the money for a bike like that?' I asked and instantly regretted it. My little brother was back; I shouldn't have come over all parental so soon.

'Belongs to a customer,' said Bruno.

Over coffee and whisky in my flat, he told me he had picked up a special airbrush technique and was now, as he put it, 'beautifying' cars and motorbikes.

'It's already going pretty well,' he said.

In fact, it never went really well—still doesn't to this day. Sometimes he earns money, sometimes he doesn't, and when he doesn't, he lives off money I give him or money his women earn, but they don't earn much and they never stick around for long either. He has fans in America, some in China, in Qatar. He gets around a lot, and he takes drugs and comes off them again. He's all right, I think. He has never wanted any other life. Sometimes I think he has it easier than I do.

Now and again I've had to send him money in Lima or Houston with Western Union, because he wouldn't have been able to get back to Germany otherwise. Once I went to Blantyre in Malawi because some people there were keeping him prisoner in a hut. He owed them a thousand dollars and didn't have a cent. But none of that makes any difference to me. He's my little brother, and I'm here for him. For a long time he was the only family I had.

He ended up moving back into the flat with Rebecca and me. It was cramped, but we got on fine; he and Rebecca like each other. After a year he found a little flat of his own in Bochum and has lived there to this day.

There's not a lot more I can say about my time in Bochum— only that, yes, there was one strange and unsettling incident.

One day—this was before mobiles—the phone rang in our flat. I picked it up, and at first I had trouble taking in the speaker's words, they were so alien to me: 'It's Dad, I was wondering how you were.' I think I was silent for a long time. In those days, I didn't know my father's telephone voice at all. He'd never rung me, not even on my birthday. My mother would ring and wish me many happy returns and tell me the story of my birth, just like the year before and the year before that. Then she would pass on a happy birthday from my father. 'Tell him thank you,' I would say. Now he was on the phone asking how I was. What was I to say?

'Fine,' I said.

'University going well?' he asked.

'Yes, great.' There was a short pause. I searched for words, but before I had found any, my father said, 'Well, that's all right then. Just wanted to know how you were.' He hung up.

When I told Rebecca, she said he was trying to send me a signal, a signal of interest.

'But he's never been interested in me,' I said.

'Yes, he has,' she said. 'You told me he took you to the firing range.'

'That's ages ago,' I said stubbornly.

A few days later, Rebecca urged me to give my father a ring, but I didn't. Today I reproach myself for that. I think he had made up his mind to rediscover his son, but found himself up against a hard heart—my heart.

I can't say I missed him during my time in Bochum, but I missed having a father. This became painfully clear to me one year after Christmas when I was waiting in Berlin for the train to take me back to Bochum. Next to me was a man of about my age who had his father with him. When the train drew into the station, the two of them hugged so hard and so long and so tearfully that it brought tears to my own eyes. I could hardly bear to look.

In the year that East and West Germany were reunited, I graduated and wanted to return to Berlin—wanted, as I said to myself at the time, to help build up the new city. Rebecca came with me and continued her studies at a prestigious research university. Even then, she knew she wasn't going to be a doctor. She was interested in the human genome, and wanted to do research in the field. We married soon afterwards, because we were sure we belonged together. Do I see things differently today? No. We belong together, although we now know that those words do not imply a good life together—certainly not consistently good.

24

ON 15 JUNE IN THE YEAR OF TIBERIUS, we held a soiree. It was, we told ourselves, a first step back to normality: we would rediscover something of the life we had lived before Dieter Tiberius. We invited the three couples we got on with the best and who knew about our situation, and one of Rebecca's schoolfriends who happened to be staying in town with his wife. We didn't know the wife. Rebecca and I agreed not to talk about Dieter Tiberius that evening. We wanted a normal evening such as we used to have, and that is what we told our friends when we invited them—but not the schoolfriend, of course, who knew nothing.

As always, Rebecca cooked a first-rate dinner, worthy of at least one star, and the evening got off to a good start. I found myself opening bottles of wine in quick succession. After dessert, we talked about a recent political scandal and about whether children were in good hands in a state school or better off going to a private school so that they might one day end up at Yale or Cambridge. Opinion was divided. Rebecca's schoolfriend's wife—who specialised in family law—was particularly vocal, declaring herself 'against the early privileging of children' and in favour of state schools, 'to allow all social classes to come into contact with each other, and to maintain that contact for as long as possible'.

I agreed to a certain extent, but said that my concern for my children's wellbeing might lead me to act 'antisocially'. This term was then hotly debated, and Rebecca was among those who disapproved of it. I opened the next bottle of Black Print, although there were already two open; as I have said, it needs time to breathe.

One of my friends now said that the real difference between the classes was the way they behaved in public. He considered it an 'admirable middle-class characteristic' that we refrained from imposing ourselves on others in everything we did. We didn't eat kebabs on the bus or the train; we didn't drink beer on the street; and even when we were drunk, we didn't urinate against trees or in alleyways.

At this point the family lawyer piped up again. She disagreed with my friend, saying how awful it was travelling on the train these days because of middle-class people talking on their mobile phones, not caring if the entire carriage heard them. Everyone had something to say to that, and the table grew loud. At around two in the morning I asked our guests to lower their voices: we did not, I said, pointing at the floor with a smug smile, want to 'disturb our dear Tiberius'. Our friends grinned, arousing the interest of Rebecca's schoolfriend, who wanted to know who this Tiberius was, and why everyone else seemed to have heard of him already.

Because I had been stupid enough to raise the topic, Rebecca abandoned our plan and told all there was to tell about Dieter Tiberius, working herself into such a rage that she even let drop the words 'our Untermensch'. I asked her several times to talk quietly, because there were only thirty centimetres separating us from Dieter Tiberius and no carpet, of course, because we have old oak parquet. Even before Rebecca had finished talking, I saw her schoolfriend's wife purse her lips. Was it not possible, she asked eventually, that Dieter Tiberius was just a victim? After all, he'd grown up a ward of the state, and we all knew what went on in children's homes.

I had not until then applied the word 'victim' to Dieter Tiberius. For us, he was the perpetrator. Even if we knew that he had probably had an awful childhood, we didn't believe that gave him the right to terrorise us. My wife said as much to the family lawyer, and then things went back and forth, getting louder and louder, and all attempts to placate the two of them failed.

The 'poor man' downstairs, said the family lawyer, had to look on daily as we 'flashed our wealth around', had to listen to us 'tottering' over the parquet in our 'Gucci shoes' and watch our children hurtling almost inevitably towards stellar careers. That must be hard to bear for a 'poor man' like him, for whom 'society' had no other plan but 'a dark, musty hole underground'. Of course he had to defend himself, said the family lawyer.

'Defend!' my wife screeched. 'We've never done anything to him.'

Oh yes, we had, said the family lawyer, we'd provoked him with our Nazi jargon.

Now I, too, had had enough and protested at this accusation.

The family lawyer said very calmly that, what was more, she knew from her work that there were also incidents of child abuse in middle-class families, and that a 'poor man' like Tiberius who was 'bound' to have been abused himself while in state care would, of course, be particularly sensitive to the issue. He would, she said, have 'special sensors'.

My wife jumped up and screamed at the lawyer to leave

the flat at once. The guest sitting next to Rebecca grabbed hold of her, otherwise there's no doubt that she would have hurled herself at the lawyer; as it was, she managed to snatch a Black Print bottle and throw it at the floor—an empty bottle that didn't shatter, but rolled away; our parquet is quite well-sprung, but not particularly even. Rebecca screamed and screamed, and then the doorbell rang.

The table fell silent immediately. It was about half past two in the morning and we hadn't called for a taxi or heard a car draw up. The woman above us had gone to stay with her daughter; the couple in the attic liked giving dinner parties themselves and had never complained about noise. I got up, went into the hall and opened the door. Dieter Tiberius said he couldn't sleep, and could we not be quieter? He didn't say it wearily, but with malice. Could he speak to my wife? he asked. She was screaming so loudly.

I saw him only indistinctly, because he hadn't switched on the light in the stairwell. He was wearing a dressing-gown that was too big for him, or at least too long; it came nearly to the floor and the sleeves almost completely concealed his hands.

He couldn't speak to my wife, I said—not coolly, I'm afraid, but enraged at his impudence.

Dieter Tiberius: 'But she's screaming so angrily.'

Me: 'I can assure you, we'll be quiet now.'

And I shut the door.

I went back into the living room and saw that some of the men, including my wife's schoolfriend, had positioned themselves protectively behind their wives' chairs. I observed it, I believe, with a scornful smile.

'Dieter Tiberius asks us to be quieter,' I said.

The conversation didn't pick up again; we tried going back to politics, but an embarrassed silence soon set in, and then my wife's schoolfriend said it was late and they would have to be getting back to their hotel. The others followed suit. I ordered taxis, and then, as we waited, made a bit of small talk—alone, because Rebecca had vanished— accepting muted compliments on the great food and the lovely evening, even from the family lawyer. When the taxis arrived, I saw our guests to the front gate, where there were hugs, handshakes and the odd surreptitious glance at Dieter Tiberius's basement. It was dark down there; he had drawn the curtains.

When I got back to the flat, my wife was sitting on the sofa. She gave the neck of the Black Print bottle a gentle kick, setting it spinning with a soft rumbling sound.

'You've got to do something,' she said. 'You've really got to do something.'

25

THE NEXT DAY, the family lawyer rang and apologised to Rebecca for her behaviour. Rebecca accepted the apology coolly and assured her that everything was fine. 'Cunt,' she said, after she'd hung up. I had never heard my wife use language like that, but I understood what had prompted it. It was galling to be told by a guest in our home that it was Dieter Tiberius who was the victim in this relationship; that we were the oppressors, and not the oppressed. A lack of compassion for the underprivileged is the last thing we're guilty of. We willingly share our good fortune with others: we sponsor a child in Africa, with whom we exchange letters; we adopted a tiger in India at Fay's request; and when there is an earthquake or some other natural disaster, we invariably make not insignificant donations.

I went to the bank that afternoon, and then I returned to the laundry. Once again I found the manager enshrouded in the steam of his machines. I offered him a hundred thousand euros for the basement flat, twice its actual value. I offered him a hundred and twenty thousand and, eventually, a hundred and fifty thousand, although my account manager had said that a hundred and twenty thousand was the maximum. We were still under considerable financial strain after buying our flat, and I am not one of those architects who get filthy rich. I do everything myself, from drafting the design to overseeing the construction, assisted by only a part-time secretary and the occasional intern. That way I am left with quite a bit of my income, but five houses is about as much as I can manage in a year. We are well-off, not rich.

'The flat's not for sale,' said the laundry manager.

'It's only a basement flat,' I said.

'For you it's only a basement flat,' said the manager, gesturing to the Moldovan woman, who switched off a machine that was hissing particularly loudly. 'I was born in that basement,' he said. 'My mother was a servant for the family who used to own the whole house. She cooked for them and did the housekeeping, and I lived there with her until I was twenty.'

He wasn't allowed upstairs with her when he was little, he said, but sat in the basement alone, listening to the footsteps of his mother and the others in the house. He had spent hours on end looking out 'from down below' at the cars and people passing by. Now part of the house belonged to him, and he wasn't going to give it up.

'Can't you turn the tenant out, at least?' I said insistently.

'What do the police say?' the laundry manager wanted to know.

'Nothing,' I said.

'I can't take the roof from over Dieter's head for no reason,' said the laundry manager. 'But if *you* want to sell, I can make you an offer.'

I ignored these last words and left.

Today I think that was the mistake of my life. I should have let our flat go. My father wouldn't be sitting in prison now and we, as a family, wouldn't have a murder on our conscience. We would have lost the battle against Dieter Tiberius and lost it unjustly, but what would that matter? I don't subscribe to the masculine ideology that rejects defeat out of hand. And yet at the same time, I didn't want to yield. For a while now, I have sometimes wondered if I didn't stay put to give my father and me a chance to reconnect—to reconnect over a crime. Is that abstruse?

When the Tiberius crisis was at its height, our son developed a twitch, pushing out his lips and wrinkling his nose in a peculiar way. He didn't do it much at first, but before long he was doing it every twenty or thirty seconds. Secretly I called it 'snouting', and this snouting was a great worry to us. Of course we blamed Dieter Tiberius—we blamed pretty much everything on Dieter Tiberius at that time. We asked Paul whether there was anything worrying him, and he said no. We asked whether he was afraid of Dieter Tiberius, and again he said no.

Paul is, in fact, an easygoing, cheerful child. He has never been difficult: he took the food we offered him, soon admitted defeat if we told him in a shop that we were not going to buy sugary treats, and when we forbade him from drawing on the wall with his felt-tips, he never did it again. Paul has my wife's dark hair and complexion, and when I mention that to her, she is kind enough to reply that he is pensive like me and has my wrists. I have narrow wrists, which means I can only wear little watches, not those massive chronometers you could hang up in a train terminal. A lot of my colleagues like to wear those watches; the more stupid among them are keen to tell you that they 'laid out' fifteen thousand euros for them, a sum of money I couldn't afford in any case. Paul has a crooked little finger, like me, like my mother. I would call Paul a gentle child, a child who often moves me because he asks on the phone: 'And how are you, Dada?'

Fay has dark hair too, but fair skin. She has my ambition, my desire to push life into the shape she wants. She is more forceful than her brother, only reluctantly took the food we gave her and never asks me how I am on the phone—but maybe she is still too little for that. She is not as pensive as her brother, but quick and direct, and often hilariously funny. At the outbreak of the Tiberius crisis, we thought she was the one we'd need to keep a close eye on, because she's prone to strong emotion and feels things so intensely, but then it was Paul who developed this strange snouting. He was having trouble with another boy at the time; the boy wasn't hitting him, but he was bullying him, and Paul no longer liked going to kindergarten. We were at a loss.

We had tried not to worry the children, despite the menace from the basement; we didn't talk about it in front of them and acted as if Dieter Tiberius didn't exist. That seemed to us the right strategy at first. Our children went on playing their games and living their lives the same as ever. We noticed no change in them—but then the snouting began. Had we done something wrong? Was there something fevered in their tireless playing? Children always keep going: even with temperatures of almost forty degrees, Fay and Paul stick their Lego bricks together as unflaggingly as ever. Had they perhaps, then, realised what state Rebecca and I were in, what danger they themselves were exposed to—and did they feel alone and anxious because nobody talked to them about it? Had Paul started the snouting out of worry or fear, even if he denied it?

I made pathetic attempts to get him to break the habit. At first I pointed it out to him in a friendly way every time he screwed up his face, and told him that he didn't have to do it, that he could stop it. As the days passed, I grew impatient, admonishing him sternly and even snapping at him. He looked guilty then, but also questioning, as if he had no idea what I wanted of him. Once I let myself get carried away to the point of exclaiming: 'Stop that snouting!' I found myself looking into big, offended eyes and apologised. But once a word is in the world, I fear it stays there.

It was not long after my unfortunate outburst—my diary tells me it was 27 June—that I went down to the basement in the evening and knocked on Dieter Tiberius's door. Nothing stirred.

'I'd like to talk to you. Please open the door,' I said. Nothing.

I went back to our living room, picked up the phone and dialled his number. I heard it ring in his flat. He did eventually answer, giving his full name.

'Randolph Tiefenthaler,' I said, adding superfluously: 'Your neighbour.'

'I don't mind going to prison,' Dieter Tiberius said at once.

I ignored this bizarre statement and made him an offer:

five thousand euros in cash plus removal costs if he left the flat within four weeks. Dieter Tiberius said he'd like to think about it, and hung up.

Money: the contemporary solution to every problem, and a contemptible one, lacking strength, grace and courage. The solution of the businessman, who has become the central figure of our civilisation. And the solution of my class: we have money, and we use that money to buy ourselves the lives we want. But there are limits, of course. I don't know why I said five thousand euros rather than ten thousand, why calculation plays a role in such matters. I could have afforded fifty thousand euros, with a bit of a struggle and maybe a loan from friends. But I said five thousand. It must, relative to my income, have been the largest sum I was prepared to put up to reward wrongdoing.

That night I pondered what he'd said about going to prison. His words frightened me, because they made him invulnerable. I realised that everything I had thought to my advantage was in fact to my disadvantage: my family, my job, my comfortable life, my money, my good reputation. I could lose all that, whereas he had nothing to lose. He lived in a dingy basement, alone and on benefits, and he was no stranger to hell, whether children's home or prison. He was tough, whereas I was timid, fearful of loss. The loser is strong because he has nothing left to lose. People like me, apparently life's winners, are weak because they have so much they want to hang on to. The upwardly mobile are particularly afraid. We are afraid of losing what we have attained, because it is not secure, neither morally nor financially. We lack the reserves, the foundations of a long family tradition.

Two days later there was a letter on the windowsill in the entryway. I tore it open, full of hope, and was disappointed: *I'm staying put. You won't get me out.* My mercantile approach had failed.

26

I NOW GOT UP EVERY MORNING thinking that I had to win my wife back, and I set about trying to impress her. I gave her detailed accounts of all the requests I had pouring in, although this was rather an excessive way to describe the actual rate at which projects were coming in—and I showed her an article in *Architectural Digest*, in which one of my houses was commended.

'I don't want you to impress me,' said Rebecca. 'I want you to inflict some normality on me—you've been depriving me. Bore me,' she said. 'Let's start with that.'

I was ashamed. It was only now that I realised I had chosen the wrong approach. It wasn't a question of my winning her back; it was a question of winning myself back for my wife. Once I had grasped this, it wasn't so hard. I told her about all I had seen and read and thought, and she did the same. Our hands found each other again when we went shopping together, and we held one another in long, spontaneous embraces that brought our arms out in goose flesh—but it wasn't Eros; it was a feeling of disconcertion at finding our bodies in such an unfamiliar situation.

What helped most was looking at things with different eyes—no longer seeing what annoyed me about my wife, but what I liked about her. I changed the story I told about my marriage and suddenly found myself with a completely different woman: not a woman who frightened me with her violent outbursts of anger, but a woman who had an outburst once or twice a year and then got over it. What mattered to me now was the time in between. It was only now that I realised the simple truth: we are not, particularly in long relationships, together with a person who really exists, but with a person we create in our heads, mainly by selecting memories. The 'real' person probably doesn't even exist. Whenever Rebecca does or says something, I see it in the context of my memories, and these can vary greatly, depending on my mood.

During this first phase of rapprochement, the two of us would often have dinner together, choosing to eat in the living room rather than the kitchen. We cooked together, or rather, I peeled what needed peeling and Rebecca took charge of anything that required skill. Then we disappeared into our bathrooms and got changed. Rebecca wore a black dress, high-heeled shoes and chunky jewellery; I wore a suit, a white shirt and a Tom Ford tie. We put out candles, Rebecca's great-grandmother's china, a wonderfully balanced Majorcan red, and talked about our everyday life, our children and whether Rebecca should take up her career again. The music was quiet enough not to disturb our conversation, but loud enough to stop Dieter Tiberius from eavesdropping and to spare us from Dustin Hoffman. I am not given to sentimentality, and I didn't let it get the better of me once in all this saga—but these evenings, when I liked to put on Shostakovich's seventh symphony, the *Leningrad*, were an exception. It was written in the besieged city and is reminiscent of military marches, especially the allegretto, a music of resilience. I approved of that at the time—cultural resistance. What nonsense, I say today.

All was well with us on those evenings. We were a normal couple, and before long we were a couple in love. Rebecca sometimes came up with strange ideas, as she had in the past. Once she said, 'Come on, let's say things to each other that no love except ours can withstand.' I wasn't sure we were quite ready for that, but I went along with it. At times like that, you can't refuse the other anything.

'You're so unsexy in the winter because you wear slippers and socks with your dressing-gown,' said Rebecca.

'But my feet are always cold in winter,' I protested.

She said cold feet were unsexy too. That hurt me; I didn't want to be unsexy, even in the winter.

'And now you have to forgive me,' said Rebecca. I swallowed my incipient resentment and forgave her, really forgave her, and I thought: What a wonderful woman.

'Now you,' said Rebecca, looking at me expectantly.

I thought for a while, but all I could come up with was: 'You breathe so loudly when you're eating.'

'Oh, come on,'—she was disappointed—'plenty of people do that; any love can withstand that.'

'Well, slippers weren't exactly original either,' I said.

'Please,' said my wife. 'Please, please, please.'

I thought, then said, 'You don't smell good when I fuck you from behind.'

That wasn't true—I loved how she smelled when we fucked—but I wanted to say something that really hurt her.

She swallowed, and I thought I'd gone too far, but then she said, 'But you still love fucking me from behind.'

'But I still love fucking you from behind,' I said.

'Because our love is so great,' she said.

'Because our love is so great,' I said. We gently clinked

our glasses of red wine.

'Ah, pass me a piece of the tomme, Ivan Ivanovich,' said Rebecca with a melancholy smile that spoke of consumption and approaching death.

'With pleasure, Anna Petrovna,' I said, cutting her a piece of cheese, 'but don't you agree that it's deathly boring here?'

'Yes,' she breathed, 'it is deathly boring, but please stop talking about character—I don't want to hear another word about character.'

I understood at once why she was talking like this; she was drawing on our seminal myth, the myth that could save us.

After dinner, Rebecca went to have a shower, which she never usually did in the late evening. When she got into bed with me, I said, 'Don't you dare wash your wonderful smell away ever again.'

'You lied,' she said. 'You're not allowed to lie if you want us to reconnect.'

Then we had sex, and I made an effort to think not of myself, but of my wife, at every moment. I daresay that doesn't sound exactly thrilling—you don't want to associate sex with effort, I know—but when you are emerging from a long, deep valley, the way up can be hard work. We both saw it that way, which made it all right.

Our children—our unabused children, for that is what they now were—grew jealous, because they weren't used to seeing their mama and dada so wrapped up in one another. In the past, they had often had me all to themselves when they were playing; now Rebecca sometimes joined us, and she and I talked to one another while I built a ship for Paul or a stable for Fay. (We are a traditional family.)

'Go away, Mama,' Fay said once, but I insisted that Rebecca stayed and soon the children, too, realised that we were a family of four.

In short, to all outward appearances, we led a normal life during those Tiberius months, living day to day as if nothing had happened, as if there were no man downstairs who was, as we saw it at the time, out to destroy our happiness. Paul stopped snouting after a couple of weeks, and we continued not to talk to the children about Dieter Tiberius, so that everything, I think, seemed normal to them.

They knew nothing of my nightly patrols around the house, and of course I never told anyone, not even my wife, about the thoughts that assailed me on those rounds— murderous thoughts. If Dieter Tiberius appeared, I would kill him, I thought, and call it self-defence. But he never did appear, and to be truthful, I was glad, not because I would otherwise have killed him, but because I probably would not have killed him, which would have revealed my defencelessness.

27

OUR LIFE WITH THE CHILDREN was not, however, all that normal. It was a while before I realised that I had stopped showing myself naked in front of Paul and Fay as a matter of course. I undressed in the bathroom and I dressed in the bathroom. When I cuddled them, I was careful not to touch them where I never touched them anyway except when I was washing them—and even that I had stopped doing. It's awful, but I can't put it any other way: whenever I washed my children, Dieter Tiberius was at my side, watching my every move.

One day he sent my wife a poem. The rhymes were primitive, but not inane; it even had a certain poetry to it. It was, largely speaking, about my wife's screams, although it was unclear whether he meant screams of anger or screams of pleasure. Rebecca is quiet in bed, on the whole, but maybe he would have liked her to scream with pleasure. Reading that was disturbing enough, but then the poem ended with his ardent desire to be present when my wife let out her final scream, after which she would 'gasp her last' and be silent for ever; here, he rhymed 'gasp her last' with 'all is past'.

'A death threat,' I said to Rebecca, my voice cracking.

She read the poem, then sat at the kitchen table in silence. 'I feel so dirty,' she said finally. 'He imagines doing all that to me, and while he's imagining it, he's close by me, almost here in the flat, like a lodger. He's a lodger in my head, too,' she said. 'In my feelings, in my body.'

'But we've got him now,' I said. 'After a death threat, the police have to take action.'

I took the letter to Ms Kröger at the crime office. She looked at it for a long time, then shook her head.

'No lawyer will see a death threat in that,' she said. 'Your neighbour's been imagining things, but there's no law against that.'

'But it's about my wife's final scream,' I cried. 'About gasping her last and all being past—it's about death.'

'Could also be sex,' she said.

'You are utterly heartless,' I said.

'Excuse me?'

'I said you are utterly heartless. You see before you a man who is afraid for his wife, afraid for his children, and all you can say is that it could also be sex.'

'I'm telling you what the law says,' she said.

I burst into tears; I admit it. They rolled down my cheeks as I shook my head, got up and left without a word. In despair, I dropped in on our lawyer, but as expected she too saw no improvement in our situation after reading the letter. I asked her where we were at with the slander charges. She said I must be patient. I withdrew the power of attorney we had granted her, and she took it indifferently.

I rang my brother, and he came round the next day. I didn't want to leave my family alone in the flat for a minute under the current circumstances. I had, it is true, almost completely transferred my office to the flat by then, but I sometimes had to drive to building sites and didn't want to take any risks.

The evening my little brother arrived we sat at the kitchen table for a long time, he and Rebecca and I, drinking red wine and not talking about Dieter Tiberius. At about midnight, Bruno went out and returned shortly afterwards with a crowbar.

'What's going on?' I asked.

'Let's get it over and done with,' he said. 'That's what I'm here for.'

'No,' I replied, 'you're not here because I want Dieter Tiberius bludgeoned to death. You're here to look after my family.'

He said he only needed the crowbar to open the bastard's door; we could do the rest with our fists. I explained to him that we were on the right side of the law and wanted to stay there.

'What's the point of a law that fails you?' my brother asked.

Today I think Dieter Tiberius might still be alive if I had listened to my little brother back then. Maybe a punch or two would have rattled him, and he would have moved out. But I don't know—I can't know. It's one of those hypothetical questions that sometimes torment me. What would have happened if I had taken a different turn in a certain situation? We always live at least two lives, especially after a big decision: the life we decided on and the life we decided against. In our minds we let that other life play out, comparing it with our actual situation. For me, that alternate life is one in which we have managed to evict Dieter Tiberius from his flat in a peaceable manner. He lives in a secure institution and cannot harm us. Now and again I go and have a cup of coffee with my father, because we have become reconciled with one another even without murder. All's well in our world.

My little brother laid the crowbar on the table and sat down. We didn't storm downstairs that evening; we had a long discussion. Bruno soon annoyed me by calling me a coward, a man who doesn't put up a fight, but only looks on as his family is attacked. I said that we might as well do away with civilisation altogether if people like me were going to resort to barbarism.

'You don't have to make such a big deal of it,' said my little brother. 'Just smash his face in—civilisation will survive.'

A violent argument ensued and old grievances were dredged up, but what really got to me was that my wife had nothing to say about it and didn't take my side. In the end I made my brother promise he wouldn't do anything without me—that he'd leave our downstairs neighbour alone. Reluctantly, he agreed.

I couldn't get to sleep for hours, as so often at that time, and in my waking dreams I saw myself as part of a great battle, as part of a civilisation that had to resist barbarism, but with its own civilised means, so that it was my duty to overcome barbarism without becoming a barbarian myself.

The next day, we had the police round again because Dieter Tiberius had reported my brother for sexually abusing our children together with my wife. Sergeant Leidinger and his colleague Rippschaft came, questioned us briefly and then left again. I told my brother he could forget his crowbar; he had given me his promise. Bruno gave me a look of contempt and disappeared back into Paul's room.

Perhaps it's hard to imagine a visit like that from the police, how it must feel. Perhaps the repetition even lends the whole thing an air of comedy, but we were unable to see it like that. Each time, we felt humiliated, besmirched, touched by evil. We were left feeling as if we had been charged but not tried. We were not guilty of any crime, but neither did we feel innocent, because we had not been found innocent; our reputation still hung in the balance. No matter how often we told ourselves we were blameless, it wasn't enough. We no longer numbered among the ranks of those whose lives are untouched by the suspicion of child abuse.

28

THE DAYS WERE NOW VERY WARM, thirty degrees, and a
blue sky hung resplendent over our sombre thoughts. One
day I was sitting in the garden, working on a model for a
house while the children played on the trampoline. It seemed
as if all was well, but I sat there like a watchman at his
post. The trampoline was behind a hedge, and I saw only
the children's heads as they popped up with laughing faces
and disappeared again. I imagined a world without them, a
world after Dieter Tiberius had snatched them from us, and

I wondered how I would live in such a world.

It was not, however, the horror that interested me in this scenario, but what solace I might find. The beauty of the mountains would remain, the beauty of the sea. My job would remain; Rebecca would remain—but would she still be the Rebecca I knew?

Paul popped up. Fay popped up. I waved at them.

When Paul was born, on a hot summer's day with the window open, my first thought was that here was a person whose life mattered more than my own, a person for whom I would give my life if it saved his. I have already written that I am not given to sentiment and it's the truth, but this was another of my rare moments of sentiment. The thought was simply there, as soon as he slid from my wife's womb. With Fay, I had the same thought, but that time it *had* to come, because there could be no difference in my love for them. There really is no difference, and it is still true: I would give my life for my children. Every father would, I hope.

I was folding the corner of a wall and spreading glue along one edge when I realised that I hadn't seen my children's heads for a while. I listened for their laughter and giggles, but heard nothing. Don't panic, I told myself. Don't be paranoid. But I was paranoid. I got up and looked behind the hedge. Paul and Fay were lying on the trampoline, blinking up at the sun in silence. I lay down next to them and closed my eyes, and we lay there like that for a while without talking.

When I opened my eyes again, I saw Dieter Tiberius at the side of the hedge with a knife in his right hand.

I leapt up, but it took me a moment to crawl out from under the safety net. Then I set off at a run. I caught a glimpse of Dieter Tiberius vanishing into the basement. Standing at the outer door, I realised that I had seen not only a knife, but also an apple: the knife in his right hand, the apple in his left. I didn't go down to the basement, didn't hammer on his door, but sat down at the garden table again and went back to working on the model. Fay came and asked me why I'd run away.

'I frightened off a fox,' I said.

'Did not,' said Fay. 'There's no fox here.'

'You're right,' I said. 'It was a slip of the tongue. I meant an ox.'

She gave me a doubtful look. 'Really?' she asked.

'Or maybe it was a unicorn,' I said.

Fay: 'But an ox is much bigger than a unicorn.'

Me: 'But not a baby ox.'

Fay: 'Is a baby ox that small?'

Me: 'Smaller than a cat, at any rate.'

Fay: 'When did you ever see a baby ox?'

Me: 'When you were born. There was one in the cot next to yours.'

Fay: 'That's not true.'

It went to and fro like this for a while. Fay went back to

the trampoline, and I turned my thoughts to possible shapes
for a bay window. You don't feel quite at ease with yourself
after you've outmanoeuvred your own child.

What had Dieter Tiberius wanted? My wife wasn't in.
He must have known that; he kept a permanent watch on
the front gate. Had he hoped that Paul and Fay were alone
on the trampoline? We were still tormented by the suspicion
that he might be after the children, although everything
he did was directed at my wife. All we had to go on was
his description of what we supposedly did to them, and we
thought, still, that only someone who lusted after children
himself could come up with such things. That was part of
our paranoia: we could only imagine the worst possibilities.
We lived a worst-case life in a worst-case world.

29

I MUST CONFESS—and this is extremely painful for me—
that I did wonder whether it was possible that my wife was
sexually abusing our children. As soon as this thought entered
my mind, I banished it; I couldn't allow Dieter Tiberius to
infect me with his perverted suspicions. And yet it happened.
I pushed the thought away a few times, but when it persisted,
I ended up acknowledging it and thinking it through to its
conclusion. I interrogated my memory thoroughly, calling to
mind scenes that took place in our bathtub—Rebecca with

Fay, Rebecca with Paul—but I could come up with nothing, nothing at all to confirm my suspicions. Try as I might, I recalled only a normal family's normal physical contact from that time, in the past now, when Dieter Tiberius had not yet frightened us into giving it up.

I realise, of course, that the world is not only what we see and hear. When our backs are turned, when we are far away, it can be a very different place. That is what makes our lives so precarious. Anything is possible in our absence, every form of betrayal, ignominy, crime—even, damn it, child abuse. I wondered what my wife did when I was out of the house, and unbearable images appeared before me. Those images made me wish Dieter Tiberius dead—yes, that's how it was, and now I've said it.

I talked of the rule of law, and it wasn't empty talk, but there were moments when I wished Dieter Tiberius dead, perhaps run over by a truck as he was crossing the road with his plastic bags. It was his fault that the images took shape in my mind; he had poisoned my thoughts. I should, I know, have been certain the images were false. I knew my wife wasn't capable of such things. I knew too that the accusations Dieter Tiberius had made against me were entirely unfounded, so the same should have applied to Rebecca. But was I certain? Let's put it like this: I forced myself into certainty.

In the latter days of this dreadful period, I was to give a

speech at a house-warming party. It's not something I like doing, but I manage: I write down what I want to say, try to calm my pounding heart by giving myself a good talking-to, and it usually goes off all right. Applause. Big thank you from the client. On such occasions I wear an elegant suit, a white shirt and a tie. People like a bit of festivity and so do I. This time I felt more agitated than usual, though. My heart was pounding in spite of the talking-to, and I stood there, looking into the upturned faces of the homeowners, a young married couple with three children, and the faces of the roofers, the carpenters, the plumbers and the electricians, whose eyes were all fixed on me expectantly—greedily, I thought, greedy for my words—and my vocal cords seized up, and my throat grew tighter and tighter, until it was too tight to let out any words.

I struggled to get those words out, but they were stuck. I couldn't dislodge them, and the roofers and plumbers were beginning to look perplexed, wondering why the man up there on his little rostrum that the carpenters had made especially for the occasion didn't get started and why he was looking so peculiar. I expect the fear that had taken hold of me was already visible. I could bear it no longer; I had to get out of there, away from those upturned faces, and I left. I didn't run; I put all my effort into controlling my pace so as to retain a last vestige of dignity. I walked past the young couple with their three children past the rows of roofers, plumbers, carpenters and electricians, who were now staring at me even harder, but nobody said a word, and then, at last, I was sitting in my car and driving off.

The next day I was to hold a small meeting in my office with some contractors, but a quarter of an hour before it was due to start, I was in such a panic that I cancelled and drove home. Only then did I tell Rebecca what had happened to me. We spent quite some time pondering the possible reason but could only come up with Dieter Tiberius. It seemed likely to us that his accusations, however far removed from reality, had triggered a sense of shame in me and a fear that people looking at me might see a child abuser.

Rebecca comforted me, reassuring me, making me cups of tea, running me baths with fragrant oils and generally being a wonderfully caring wife, but there was no improvement. I couldn't speak to more than three people at once. I was jeopardising my job, or so I thought at the time. An architect doesn't have to be a public speaker, but he does have to make the odd speech, and to negotiate and contend with contractors and clients—and I no longer could. If I had so far applied the word 'weakling' to myself, it was with a certain self-deprecating pride—we intellectual types are, after all, the true strongmen in a democracy, in a society where the law prevails—but now I truly felt like a weakling, completely at the mercy of Dieter Tiberius.

Twice I went to a therapist, who soon found out that

my father is an interesting case and kept wanting to talk to me about him, because, as he put it, we had to 'get to the root causes', but I didn't feel this line of inquiry would get me anywhere. His remark that I should stop 'going out of my way' to regard my childhood as normal was equally unhelpful. I got him to prescribe me tranquillisers and didn't go back. The tranquillisers helped, but because they were addictive I only took them sparingly, and after a few weeks I realised that I no longer needed them. I felt a little insecure before meetings, but I was able to get through them without anybody noticing anything.

It was then that I first understood my father's fears. I still didn't know where they came from, but I knew how they worked. They appear suddenly, seemingly without reason, pulling themselves down over your mind like a black hood, taking hold completely and yelling: 'Run away!' Inside, you become a quivering creature, a deer scenting wolves without seeing them. You are divided. Even as you sit or stand somewhere, you are already gone, running, tearing away, escaping your own body. Unbearable tension; it tears you apart. And shame, great shame, at being such a lousy fucking deer.

I understood that my father couldn't bear his fears, and that the guns were his protection against them. Tormented by inner demons, he could only feel safe by convincing himself that it was external threats he feared. Guns could keep him safe from the criminals he saw in the papers and on the news, making him feel secure. Those demons are something I'll have to ask him about when he's out of prison—soon, then, with any luck. Maybe it was something that happened to him during the war after all, even though he never told stories as horrific as my mother's. Maybe it was his father. A father is always a good place to look for a demon.

It was then that I began to tell my mother about our troubles over the phone. Until that time I had spared her, making a nasty clown out of Dieter Tiberius rather than a threat. Now I made myself clearer, telling her about the letters we'd found on the windowsill. He had now written three poems about my wife, all revolving around sex and death.

At the same time, as I have said, family life carried on as usual. We went on outings to the Spree Woods, a landscape I love more than any other in the world: narrow streams between tall poplars that bend towards one another to make a vast natural cathedral. We hired two canoes and toured the labyrinth of waterways between green meadows, Fay in a boat with me, Paul with Rebecca. The paddles splashed in the water, and I told stories about Lieutenant Shivkov, an officer of the LAPD I had invented for the children, or we sat and watched for beavers in wily silence, and sometimes we saw one, to the children's great delight. We let them play at a water park, while we lay on the grass and held each other tight, almost having sex, but not really; we were, as an American friend of mine would say, too 'prudey' for that. Rebecca told me what she'd most like to do to me and I told her what I'd most like to do to her. Every now and then the children came and poured cold water down our necks.

On the drive home, when Paul and Fay were asleep in the back of the car, Rebecca said there was nothing she wanted more than for Tiberius to disappear, but that sometimes the thought frightened her.

'Because you're afraid I'd disappear inside myself again?' I asked.

'Yes,' she said, 'you might disappear again once the danger was over.'

I assured her it wouldn't happen, but I knew myself how tenuous statements about the future are. I too was aware that our happiness with one another was a happiness bestowed on us by Dieter Tiberius. Did that mean it was bound up with him? It was bad enough, I thought, that Dieter Tiberius had brought us so much trouble, but it was somehow even worse that he had brought us happiness: the restoration of our marriage and of a good family life. Can evil beget goodness? And what is the goodness worth, if it owes its very existence to evil? Does such goodness evaporate when the evil disappears? I made no real attempt to answer these questions.

One evening when my little brother was out, Rebecca and

I sat in the living room having one of what we now called our 'big evenings'—good food, smart clothes, Shostakovich, good conversation—and after the main course, she said, 'I have to ask you something, but you mustn't be angry with me.'

'Of course, you can ask me anything,' I said, unsuspectingly.

'The last time we were on holiday in Minorca,' Rebecca said, 'why did you lie on the sofa with Fay naked?'

I knew exactly what she was talking about. We had spent a day at the beach—bathing with the children, swimming out to sea, sandcastles, frisbee, books with sand between the pages, newspapers crumpled up by the wind, suncream, snuggling up on blankets, more bathing. When it got cooler, I took Fay back to the house; she was exhausted after the long day and had begun to shiver.

'Take your wet things off,' Rebecca called after us. We did. Fay was properly trembling by then, and we quickly got under a blanket on the sofa. Fay immediately fell asleep, and before long I too was asleep. We woke up when Paul pulled the blanket off us.

'I told you to take your wet things off,' said Rebecca now, 'so that you wouldn't catch cold, and yet for a moment I was disturbed to see you both naked on the sofa.'

'Fay was so cold,' I said. 'I wanted to get her under the warm blanket straight away.' I said it like a defendant trying to demonstrate his innocence. I told my wife that I wasn't a fucking child molester. So there we were. I didn't like her now, because she suspected me of something I myself had suspected her of.

Strangely enough, it had never occurred to me that Rebecca might have wondered about me, just as I had wondered about her. It pained me now. I was pained by the suspicion itself, and by the thought of the disgusting things my wife had pictured me doing with our children.

'Forgive me, please,' said Rebecca. 'I trust you. I just wanted to have talked to you about it.'

'I trust you, too,' I said. It should be a beautiful moment, a sublime moment, when two people exchange words like these, but we were forced to express our trust where there should have been no need. 'I trust you not to abuse our children' is something you should never have to say. We sat there together, deeply unhappy, two confirmed non-abusers.

When my little brother came home we were still sitting in the living room. I don't know whether we had spoken in the meantime. We were wrapped up in our black thoughts, engrossed in our life under Tiberius. Bruno tried to cheer us up, but he didn't get anywhere, and we all three sat there in silence until we went to bed.

30

WE SOON RECEIVED ANOTHER LETTER from Dieter
Tiberius, accusing us of having stolen his bike. A laughable
accusation—we all had Bianchi bikes, because I'm so fond
of the celeste green used by that brand, and he had a rusty,
rickety ladies' bike—but the blatant abstruseness of the charge
did nothing to reassure me. I saw in it further evidence of
the man's madness—a madness that would stop at nothing.
Every ring at the door set off warning signals in my head:
Is that him? I shooed the children into their rooms before

opening the door, muscles tensed as if for a boxing match, and soon afterwards, feeling relieved but rather sheepish, found myself signing my name with the electronic pen the DHL man hands you when you accept a parcel.

Then a letter came from Dieter Tiberius in which he took back all accusations—bicycle theft and child abuse— and apologised. We did not celebrate, too sceptical for that, but for the first time in ages we felt hope again. The next day we got another letter. He took nothing back: everything was true, and the situation, he wrote, was getting worse and worse. The police came and went.

We found ourselves a new lawyer, an older, experienced man recommended to us by friends. He was understanding and somehow had a more constructive way of frustrating our hopes. We shouldn't expect too much from the slander charges, he said. He'd have no trouble convincing a judge that Dieter Tiberius had badly slandered us, but the penalty would only be a fine, which wouldn't even hurt him because he'd be too poor to pay it. He'd have to do a bit of community work, but would stay in his flat. That destroyed our last shred of faith in the law. I spent a lot of time on the phone to my mother.

'Listen,' my little brother said to me one day, 'if you don't want to smoke that guy down there out of his hole yourself, then let someone else do it, but stop putting up with all this like such a wuss.'

He knew people, customers of his, who could do the job. They'd let the freak have it, he said, and nobody would be able to prove that we were behind it. It would very much surprise him if 'that bastard' decided to stay after 'treatment' of that kind, and if he did, he'd just have to have a 'second lot'.

I had been pondering this method for a while. I'd been calling it the 'Chechen solution', ever since a client of mine, a Georgian, on hearing the rough outline of our story, had suggested leaving the matter to 'Chechen friends' of his. I hadn't taken him up on this, of course, but in the back of my mind, the Chechen solution sometimes surfaced—as a solace, or a revenge fantasy.

When my brother spoke to me I was too worn down to say no firmly. First I said no, then I let myself get drawn into a discussion, and in the end I agreed to go and see these people. Bruno made some phone calls, and when he was done we had an appointment that evening with a man who called himself Mickel.

We drove to the north-east of Berlin. My little brother directed me to a bar with a great many motorbikes parked outside, mostly heavy motorbikes and choppers. I saw that two of them had been decorated by Bruno with women and warriors from fantasy worlds.

'Are you proud of me?' Bruno asked as we stood in front of them.

'Yes,' I said, 'I'm proud of you.'

The bar was called the Fuzz. The man who called himself Mickel was sitting at a table right at the back, by the wall. We crossed a dark smoky room. All the tables were full; a few people were throwing darts at a target. Mickel was a thin man of about sixty—pointed nose, narrow lips, white eyelashes, white eyebrows, his skull bald except for a wreath of white hair hanging down in long strands. He was wearing a heavy sleeveless vest, like rockers wear. Almost everyone in the Fuzz was wearing them, even the few women. Rock music blared out of the speakers. Beer was put down in front of us, although we hadn't ordered any.

'You've got a problem,' said Mickel to me in broad Berlin dialect. 'Tell me about it.'

I gave him a detailed and rather dramatic report on Dieter Tiberius. When I was finished, Mickel said briefly: 'That'll be a thousand euros, plus two hundred expenses.'

'But I don't want him to get injured,' I said.

'That'll cost you one thousand five hundred,' said Mickel, 'plus three hundred expenses, because of the towels.'

'Why towels?' I asked and saw my little brother roll his eyes.

'To wrap up their fists,' said Mickel.

I wanted to know why a gentle treatment was so much more expensive than a rough one, and Mickel explained in some detail how complicated it was to hurt people without injuring them.

A woman came up to the table—short skirt, low cleavage, red shoes. She put down a bundle of banknotes and Mickel moistened a finger and counted them. I counted too; it must have been about nine hundred euros. Mickel nodded, the woman left.

'My big brother wants to preserve civilisation,' Bruno said.

'And we're to help him?' Mickel asked.

I was annoyed. Everything had been going well; why did Bruno have to show me up now?

'We could try sticking to the Geneva Convention,' said Mickel.

I was still marvelling that he'd even heard of the Geneva Convention when my brother said, 'Take along the International Committee of the Red Cross and a couple of paramedics and you can't go wrong.'

'Cost you extra, though,' said Mickel, and Bruno laughed.

'You're such an arsehole,' I snapped at him.

'Can't you see what a fool you're making of yourself?' he snarled, coming very close to me. 'If you can't act like a man then at least let others act like men.'

I headbutted him hard in the forehead; I couldn't stop myself. We both jumped up, knocking over our beer glasses, and started wrestling, but only seconds later I found myself in the firm grip of a rocker; Bruno likewise. Mickel gave us a medium-weight slap round the head, more from solicitude than in anger, and told us to piss off; he couldn't do business with people like us.

Outside, my brother gave one of the motorbikes he'd decorated a kick. It fell over with a crash and we ran away laughing, jumped into my car and drove off with screeching tyres.

The next day my brother heard that the motorbike was seriously damaged, and Mickel's lads were looking for him. He went to Qingdao for a while to decorate a Bentley for a rich Chinese client.

31

WHEN I RETURNED TO BERLIN after graduating, I began by working in the office of an established architect. Three years later I went freelance, rented a few rooms in a nice part of the city, made some investments and suddenly found myself with a pile of debts. I specialised in family homes, starting off with major renovations and conversions and then gradually designing more and more houses myself. Nothing was left of my fantasies of building a new world, but we all grow older, and I found it gratifying to be able to provide other people with a home. In no other area of architecture is the owners' happiness as palpable as in mine. How pleased they are to have made themselves a home for life—although often enough, of course, this is not the case. I have sometimes rebuilt houses of my own design for a new family after the first family has broken up.

I was good at my job and won a few prizes. My favourite work? A house in Dahlem, entirely of glass: rectangular, two storeys, with a panel of horizontal slats running along the top, three centimetres apart. The visible undersides of the slats are painted in various colours, making the house appear not garish but colourful and vibrant, and always different, depending on your angle of vision and the position of the sun. That is the house that was praised in *Architectural Digest*.

Rebecca graduated and got a job as research assistant to a professor who was working on the Human Genome Project. The aim of the project was to decode the human blueprint, but also to get rich and famous; there were hopes that genetic research would yield breakthroughs leading to new drugs. Rebecca's professor was sequencing chromosome 21, which promised to be particularly lucrative. Rebecca was good at her job and worked hard, but so did I, and we meant enough to one another not to drift apart.

It was only in 1998 that things got tough, when Craig Venter caused a furore. Does anyone remember Craig Venter? He's the American who founded the company Celera

Genomics and was able to decode human DNA quickly using a special method, focusing above all on those sections that promised to be profitable—so chromosome 21, among others. A race began, a race for fame and patents. Rebecca had to work even at the weekend, and when she did have time off, she was drained and not particularly sociable. Before we knew it, we were in the middle of our first crisis.

Sometimes we argued too, because I refused to accept that humans are determined by their genes. I believe humans are autonomous beings, master of our own decisions. That may sound naive; I know there are people who aren't free to do what they want. But essentially, my view can be summed up as follows: *We have the choice.* Rebecca, naturally enough, sees things differently. For her, our genes are a major force, with considerable influence over our lives.

'But look at my brother and sister and me,' I once said. 'We're made up of the same genes, and yet we're completely different people.'

'Has it ever occurred to you,' she asked, 'that you're an architect, your brother decorates motorbikes and your sister studied fashion design—that you all three draw and paint although you're supposedly so different?'

'But our parents don't draw and paint,' I said stubbornly.

'You're blind,' Rebecca said. 'Did anyone ever knit more beautiful jumpers for her children than your mother? I've seen all the pictures in the family albums,' she continued.

'There's talent there—the urge to express oneself in pattern and form—design as a manifestation of love.'

'But I haven't inherited anything from my father,' I said, and the answer flung back at me was the answer I have heard so often in this context.

'That's because you don't *want* to have inherited anything from your father. But they're good genes,' said Rebecca. 'They're genes that could tell you how to enjoy a long marriage, how to provide for your children in difficult times—'

'I'll provide for my children too,' I said, interrupting Rebecca—foolishly, as it turned out.

'Exactly,' she said, not skipping a beat, 'it's all there inside you, even before you've had children of your own.'

I had been defeated once again and I was annoyed, but didn't give up. At the end of these discussions we usually agreed that our lives are like a Greek tragedy: the gods guide and steer the humans, but in the end it's the humans themselves who make the decisions.

'So they do have the choice,' I always said, despite myself.

'They choose the way God wills,' Rebecca would say, and I always suspected that this was not an empty phrase, but a cunning way to show me she had been right all along—only I never managed to work out where the cunning lay.

In the middle of the hottest phase of sequencing, Rebecca got pregnant. We had never really used contraception. I took care, she took care, except that now one of us—or both of us—hadn't. It was clear to her that she should have an abortion; it was less clear to me. We had long discussions about what our life would be like if we had a child—in my view, very nice; in hers, not at all, because she would be prevented from working full time just as things were getting exciting. But then she couldn't bring herself to have the abortion after all. Paul was born, and six weeks after his birth, his mother was sequencing again.

We had made logistically complicated breast-pumping and childcare arrangements, but they didn't go well. Rebecca's professor, driven by the desire for immortal fame, was dissatisfied because Rebecca couldn't give her work 'everything'. Rebecca was unhappy because she missed her baby when she was at work and missed her work when she was with the baby. Perhaps she hoped that I would cut back my working hours to allow her to do more, because I was the only person she really trusted with the baby. But I was already earning good money, and she, as is the way of the world, wasn't. That, I thought, put paid to that solution and, after lengthy discussions, she thought so too. Six months later she gave up and took maternity leave. She never returned to her job.

A sad story? Rebecca gets cross at our soirees when career women, who are so sure they have made the right choices, express pity for her; we have had some nasty arguments. The women go for each other's throats; the men grow more and more taciturn. But I also know that Rebecca is often bitter at having missed her chances of a career. I comfort her by saying that there is nothing more commendable than to dedicate your life to your children, but I know it's easy to say that if you are a man who has been (and still is) able to spread his wings professionally. Lately, Rebecca has talked a lot about wanting to go back to work.

Through the children, we got to know each other all over again, because children change everything, especially their parents. After the first few months with Paul, it was clear which of us had the strength to sit up with a sick baby three nights in a row and which of us didn't. (I didn't, Rebecca did.) We fought so many battles in those early years that we no longer knew whether we were still partners or had become opponents. It was the allocation of time that was at issue: who could leave the screaming baby to the other one and go out for a glass of wine? Who got to go to Barcelona with an old schoolfriend at the weekend?

We now knew what it was not to want each other at night, because you'd spent more or less all day with a baby in your arms, on your belly, on your chest, and any further human contact would send you over the edge. Maybe that was another reason we drifted apart. But I resist this thought, because children are the best that can happen to us, and how should anything negative come of the best? On the other hand, if evil can beget goodness, then presumably goodness can also beget evil. We have to live with these inconsistencies.

I grew closer to my parents when the children were babies, especially to my mother, who is a marvellous grandmother. My father doesn't make a bad job of things either; sometimes this gives me a strange feeling, which I would be horrified to think of as jealousy. Just as we can tell different stories about our partners, we can, I suppose, also tell different stories about our parents.

About six months after my sister died, I got a phone call from my mother. I clearly remember that it was a Tuesday; I was on a building site wrangling with some bricklayers when my mobile rang, and it was my mother shouting excitedly that my father was at the gynaecologist's. I knew at once what she meant. The gynaecologist has been our family's enemy ever since he overlooked Cornelia's breast cancer.

'I've had a call from the receptionist,' my mother said.

I left the wrangling bricklayers, ran to my car and sped off. I knew where the practice was and, although a law-abiding citizen who even has trouble jaywalking, I ignored every traffic signal, every road sign that didn't speed my progress. I had always believed my father capable of a massacre. Whenever I heard on the news that there had been a killing spree, I would hold my breath, unable to relax until it was clear that it couldn't have been him. That's paranoid, I know, but it's inevitable if you grew up the way I did. Already I could see the corpses piled up in Cornelia's gynaecologist's practice and the blood flowing in broad streams. I double-parked, ran up the stairs three at a time and prayed, although I'd stopped praying years ago, that I wouldn't hear shots now, at the last second.

'Where's my father?' I cried to the receptionist and she pointed into the waiting room. There he was, sitting on a chair, his arms folded in front of his chest. On his left was a pregnant woman; on his right a woman breastfeeding her baby. In a corner, a child was playing with wooden blocks. The waiting room was two-thirds full—a dozen women. My father didn't see me—or rather, he didn't register my presence; he was staring into space. When I touched him on the shoulder, he jumped slightly, but not enough to reach for his gun.

'It's me,' I said.

'Randolph,' he said.

'Come on, let's go home,' I said. I took hold of his right arm, as if to help him up, but in fact to prevent him from pulling his gun; he had it with him, no doubt about it. He got up, very slowly, like a much older man. The women looked at us as I led my father out, little step by little step.

On the stairs he began to cry. I had never seen my father cry and didn't know what to do. Then he flung his arms around my neck, which he had never done before either, and sobbed into my skin; I could feel his tears. I was, I must confess, helpless, overwhelmed. I wanted to free myself from his clasp

244

and run away, but I was his son; I couldn't abandon him.

I could feel the revolver under his armpit.

'Give me the gun,' I said, although it was unnecessary; he wasn't going to start a massacre now. It was my way of resolving the situation, putting an end to the embrace. Obediently he stepped back half a pace, fumbled around, brought out the revolver and handed it to me. Because I had heard someone coming in the door, I stuck the revolver into the waistband of my trousers, under my jacket, and led my father down the stairs, still sobbing. A woman gave us a funny look; the revolver was pressing against my coccyx.

We got into my car and I dropped my father off at home, and then drove back to the building site, strangely agitated, I must say, because if my father had toyed with the idea of shooting the gynaecologist or even starting a massacre at his practice, it could only mean that he had loved his daughter. That hadn't been clear to us when she was alive. Hidden love.

What did this tell us about my father's feelings towards my little brother and me? Were we loved too? I couldn't follow this thought through to its conclusion, seized with fear of my emotions. It was clear to me, though, that my father was capable of a great deal if anything bad happened to one of his children. Today I know that my father loves me—that he has always loved me. Men of his generation love in a different way from us; they love without showing it.

I do things differently with Paul and Fay. For a long

time, I thought I had escaped my father. I wasn't particularly interested in cars, I wasn't a salesman, I didn't work for Ford, I was a completely different kind of person. That, I thought, had always been my advantage. An intelligent woman like Rebecca could hardly avoid following her mother into medicine. For me, the field was free; I didn't have to do what my father did, because I had repudiated my father. I thought I was free. What a fool. We can't escape our parents. We go their way, or we go another way because we don't want to go theirs. Even with my own children, I am my father's son, acting in a particular way because he acted otherwise. Nothing is as deeply lodged in us as our parents; there's no shaking them off. It took me a long time to understand that. At our soirees, there is no greater, no more emotive topic than parents. There are moments when it can turn fifty-year-olds into children, crying over wounds incurred forty-five years ago, longing to hear words that haven't been spoken since, and hankering—desperately hankering—to be cradled in Mum or Dad's arms, then and there.

32

I SAW DIETER TIBERIUS IN the garden another two or three times. He kept his distance, hanging around his door and beating a retreat whenever I got up out of the deckchair. I never saw him with a knife again, or an apple. 'Clear off,' I called out to him. He said he was allowed to be there, and from a legal point of view, he was right. From then on, I made do with getting up from time to time, to put an end to his unbearable presence. The children bounced on the trampoline, oblivious.

I had told a friend about the knife episode—without, however, mentioning the apple. It was ridiculous to leave out that detail, but I increasingly had the impression that other people regarded our situation as rather less dramatic than we did, because nothing dramatic had happened. They had no idea of our silent terror, the terror of our own thoughts. That's why I left out the apple—so as to be understood, at last. Instead my friend thought the situation so dramatic that he was convinced we ought to move out at once. What's more, he couldn't believe that the law wouldn't intervene when someone lunged at you with a knife.

'He didn't exactly lunge at us,' I said, realising that I had made a mistake—that the drama of our situation lay in being threatened in an undramatic fashion. I stopped telling my friends about Dieter Tiberius. If they asked, I gave vague, laconic answers. 'Nothing new,' I would say.

In August we spent three weeks in Minorca again. It was a good holiday to begin with, and our unabused children were cheerful—not that they weren't cheerful at home—but then something happened that saddened Rebecca and me. Walking back to our house from the beach one day in the late afternoon, laden with towels, empty picnic basket, water wings and so on, we passed, as we did every day, a low stone wall. In one place there was a hole at the bottom and the children stopped to puzzle over it. Why was it there?

'For animals,' said Fay, which we all thought seemed

plausible. We came up with some animals that would be able to creep through the hole: cats, dogs, foxes—if there were foxes in Minorca—martens...

'Crocodiles,' I said.

'There aren't any here,' said Paul knowledgeably.

'There are lambs, though,' crowed Fay.

Then Paul said, 'But Tiberius wouldn't fit through there.'

That came as a shock. It was the third week of our holiday; we had hardly mentioned Dieter Tiberius, and of course we hadn't mentioned him at all in front of the children. What had made Paul think of him now? What was going on in my boy's head?

'No,' I said quickly, 'he's too fat.'

'He's really fat,' said Paul.

'Completely fat', said Fay.

'He's not here anyway,' said Rebecca, and I heard a quaver in her voice. We went back to talking about animals: moles, mice...

In the evening, when the children were in bed, my wife and I sat on the terrace, drinking wine and talking about whether it was right to avoid mentioning Dieter Tiberius to the children. I felt that our strategy had failed; Paul's words made it clear that the children had not forgotten the threat— that it was still working away inside them and occasionally broke out.

'We should have called in a child psychologist,' I said.

'They'd cope better with Dieter Tiberius then.'

A bird called in the night, an annoying call, regular, insistent; later we heard our neighbours bang spoons against pans to drive the bird away, but it wasn't to be scared off. We were silent for a long while, and I let myself be carried away by the appalling idea that my children might fall into Dieter Tiberius's clutches, be kidnapped, locked up, abused. These thoughts were punctuated by happier images: Fay snuggled up with her cuddly toys, Paul on the floor with his Brio train set. I saw them trapped underground, thinking back to those happy, carefree days. We lay awake a long time that night. I heard Rebecca toss and turn, heard the bird call.

When we got home, there was a letter with a poem on the windowsill. I didn't even read it properly—just skimmed it to see what Dieter Tiberius had come up with this time, and then took it to our lawyer, a routine procedure conducted without hope. There was still no date for the hearing into the slander charge, but that was almost irrelevant. I rang my mother. I told her about what Paul had said in Minorca and described our hopeless situation. This marked a turning point in our relationship. It was my job to provide my mother with happy stories. Her daughter was dead; her younger son shocked her with his lifestyle and she couldn't possibly imagine him happy, even though he was. My life, on the other hand, corresponded with her idea of success: a stable family, wealth, a certain standing.

'Are *you* happy at least?' she would sometimes ask, after lamenting Cornelia's death and Bruno's putative unhappiness at some length—and so far, I had always given her the same answer: 'Yes, Mum, I'm happy.' Then I would supply her with stories of my successful life, even in the days when my marriage was by no means a model of success. I was the purveyor of happiness; I couldn't afford to be reckless and tell her the truth.

Now I supplied my mother with reports of unhappiness from the World of Tiberius. I can't recall planning this; it just happened. I began to make those phone calls and only gradually did it dawn on me that I was pursuing a goal. Looking back on it today, I think that a strategy had begun to take shape in the deepest well of my subconscious, right down at the bottom, in the stagnant water where toads guard our forbidden thoughts. Sometimes the toads let these thoughts rise up in the water—let them bubble up and ferment until they become deeds. I suppose that's how it was with me. I knew that my mother would tell my father everything I told her. I knew how much it would upset my father, because I had seen him in Cornelia's gynaecologist's practice. Perhaps a faint hope stirred in me that he wouldn't put up with it for long, but I can't say any of this was consciously thought out.

One morning Dieter Tiberius rang me on my mobile. He had the number from better days, when he had once asked me for advice because something in his flat was broken.

'Are you still talking to me?' he asked abruptly.

'Yes,' I said in alarm, hoping, perhaps, that there was a suitable solution after all.

'Do you believe,' asked Dieter Tiberius, 'that nothing I have seen or heard has taken place?'

My reply, soured by my initial disappointment, was rather ridiculous: 'I'll only discuss that in court.'

He paused a long while, then said, 'When you were at my door, you said I needed help, because I'm sick, but I'm not sure that's the case.'

'I am certain that you're sick and need help,' I said.

'Do you believe,' he continued, 'that there isn't a single accurate detail in what I've said?'

There was only one reply to that: 'No, not the slightest detail.'

He was silent again.

'You should seek help,' I said, more mildly now.

'Sometimes I'm not sure,' he said. 'Maybe I really am sick. I'd like to go to the doctor some time, but I'm always scared.'

I promised to find a doctor for him, and then we hung up.

I asked my GP whether he had a colleague with a background in psychology. He recommended someone, and I soon had the psychotherapist's promise that he would visit Dieter Tiberius. An appointment was duly made; I saw the doctor draw up in his car, get out and press Dieter Tiberius's buzzer at the front gate. There was no response. I heard the doctor press the buzzer several times, until eventually I opened the gate and let him in the front door. We went down to the basement together, rang, banged, called—in vain. I thanked the doctor and apologised to him and off he went, taking with him my last hope of a peaceable solution. The next day there was another poem on the windowsill.

33

WHAT HAPPENED NEXT, I described at the beginning, or more or less. Our front gate has always squeaked; even oiling it was no use, and so it squeaked too when Dieter Tiberius's body was carried out to the street. I stood at the window watching, without triumph, but relieved. My father had already been taken away by then. I rang Rebecca, then my mother. Neither seemed surprised. We didn't talk about the crime or the events leading up to it; our thoughts were focused on Dad—how we could help him, how we could make his life in custody easier.

In the course of the investigations, the detective superintendent briefly pursued the idea that the whole thing was a family conspiracy, a murder plot, but we assured him that not a word had been spoken on the matter, and that wasn't a lie. I really had never talked to my father about Dieter Tiberius; we spoke to each other only once during all this time, on his birthday, and not much was said on that occasion beside 'Many happy returns' and 'Thank you very much' and 'How are you?' and 'Very well, and you?' and 'Very well too' and 'Take care' and 'You too.' The way it was between my father and me. Nor did I ever suggest to my mother that she should speak to my father, and Rebecca wasn't privy to my plan, if you can even call it a plan. We communicated with one another differently, silently, the way our family does. Everybody understood the signals, and silent consensus is not punishable; it is, in any case, not provable. What tipped the scales was that my father accepted all guilt and denied any conspiracy. The detective superintendent did not pursue his suspicion any further. I don't know whether he believed us. He must have realised he wouldn't find any evidence.

In March of the following year the trial began. I was nervous. We knew the prosecutor would bring charges of murder, but our lawyer allowed us to hope that the jury might in the end come to the conclusion that it was manslaughter. You get life for murder, and serve a minimum of at least fifteen years. For manslaughter, you get fifteen years maximum and serve a minimum of seven and a half years. The question was whether my father, then seventy-seven years old, would ever live as a free man again.

The jury was chaired by a blond woman in her mid-fifties with a round, friendly face, a voluminous hairdo that nearly doubled the size of her head—the kind of hairdo I hate sitting behind in the theatre—and clunky gold jewellery. The prosecutor, in his early fifties, was gaunt, almost emaciated. I could see him running marathons. He charged my father with murder, because malice aforethought, the defining characteristic of murder, was present. Some spectators hissed when they heard that. The courtroom was almost full; the press had reported the case in detail, and largely with understanding. The greatest goodwill, I am afraid to say, was expressed by the papers I didn't normally read, but which now became my allies. A family under threat taking the law into their own hands fitted their world view, and I began to read the tabloids with new sympathy. Today I would cite this as an additional sign—along with my arrogant language and altered mindset—of the barbarism into which Dieter Tiberius had plunged us. The crime itself, of course, was also barbaric.

At the beginning of the trial, my father made a confession. Unlike me, he's good at speaking. He gave a powerful description of the fear he had felt for his grandchildren, son and daughter-in-law, of the unbearable notion that something might happen to his loved ones at the hands of that 'man in the cellar'. He spoke angrily of the impotence of the authorities, of a state that had not been capable of protecting an innocent family who had done nothing wrong. If I am not mistaken, the judge and the prosecutor looked embarrassed at that.

'I am guilty,' my father said at the end of his speech. 'I killed somebody because I didn't know how else to help my family. I must be punished for that and I will bear my punishment with humility.'

My father kept his cool and for that I admire him. He said nothing about the exact circumstances of the crime.

Hardly had he reached the end of his statement when the door of the courtroom opened and a man in a hoodie came in. The hood was pulled down so low over his face that it was a while before I recognised my little brother. I motioned to him to sit down next to me, but he found himself a seat at the edge. I hadn't seen him since he left for Qingdao; my emails had gone unanswered. I was pleased that he'd come, but surprised at his unfriendly glances.

That morning, Rebecca was the first witness to testify. She described her fears for herself and her children, the suffering inflicted on her by the letters and poems. She did it very well, appearing unfazed, but not cool—troubled by her horrific memories without succumbing to emotion. Our lawyer insisted on reading out all Tiberius's missives. As he did, I could feel the shock in the courtroom.

After Rebecca, it was my turn. I too spoke of our fears and gave a detailed account of my efforts to solve the problem by legal means. I constructed my entire testimony around the word 'defenceless'. We had been defenceless; we had suffered as a result of our defencelessness. The state, which had our trust, our taxes (which we paid regularly) and our allegiance (which we demonstrated by voting in every election), had left us defenceless. I was not quite as unfazed as Rebecca; my voice occasionally trembled. But I didn't make a bad job of it. Now and then I glanced at my little brother, but I couldn't catch his eye because he had his head propped in his hands and was staring at the floor.

The prosecutor pestered me with questions for a while. Why, he asked, hadn't we simply moved out?

'Would you give up your home if you were being threatened by someone who was entirely in the wrong?' I retorted.

'I certainly wouldn't solve the problem with murder,' said the prosecutor.

At that our lawyer intervened: 'Are you insinuating that the witness committed a murder?'

The prosecutor was not, he said, insinuating anything.

The presiding judge urged them to keep a neutral tone and asked the prosecutor whether he had any further questions to put to the witness.

'No further questions,' said the prosecutor.

In the recess, I went straight to my brother. I wanted to give him a big loving hug, the way I always did, but he was stiff and awkward, his body rejecting my embrace. Disappointed, I let him go, because Rebecca was waiting to hug him too, and I saw the two of them hold each other long and affectionately.

'Why the hood?' Rebecca wanted to know, and my little brother said that they were always trying one or another of Mickel's gang here in the local criminal court, and he had to reckon on running into them. They were still angry with him.

We went to a pub across the road from the court, and even before the sandwiches and coffee had come, my brother asked me in a sullen, almost offensive tone: 'Why did you have to drag Dad into this? Why couldn't you do it yourself?'

I said that I hadn't dragged him into it, that I had never talked to our father about murder, that I hadn't talked to him at all at that time. 'You know him,' I said.

'Stop taking the piss,' said my little brother. 'We both know you dragged him into it.'

I only weakly denied it this time.

'Why weren't you man enough to deal with it yourself?' he asked, in the same sullen tone. I said that this was the best solution for the family. If I'd done it, Paul and Fay would have lost not only their breadwinner, but also their father, their companion. They too would have grown up fatherless.

'What do you mean, *they too?*' my brother hissed, stressing the word 'too'.

'Like us,' I said.

He hadn't grown up without a father, Bruno said. His tone was snotty now, not sullen.

Our father, I said, never did anything for me. Now he'd had the chance to do something for me and he had taken it.

'Coward,' said my brother, far too loud.

Sitting at the next table were some judges or lawyers in their robes; a few of them turned around and my little brother stuck up his finger at them. Rebecca laid a hand on Bruno's forearm and said: 'Sssh.' Our food arrived, and we ate in silence until my little brother started to tell us about his experiences in China. Then we went back across the road, and the second part of the first day of the hearing began.

My father's sizeable stockpile of weapons played an important role at the trial. The prosecutor initially saw it as evidence of 'a propensity to violence', but then a psychologist spoke as an expert witness in my father's defence. This man made an excellent impression on me, portraying my father as a somewhat comical figure, but by no means a fool—someone who 'owing to unprocessed and even denied war traumas' had 'a disproportionate need of security, accompanied by a desire for violence'—a desire which was not, however, 'directed towards fulfilment'.

My father was, the psychologist said, able to 'keep his fantasies of killing—fantasies common to a great many people—confined to his head without any trouble', but there was no doubt that he was 'dangerous in a state of complete helplessness, because he had only to enact what he had so often imagined, and because his fears rid him of inhibitions'. His family's predicament had put him in just such a state; it had been the trigger that had 'transported Hermann Tiefenthaler's propensity to violence out of his fantasy world and into reality'. I had no idea whether or not that was true, but it sounded good in a convoluted kind of way and delivered my father from the stigma of that 'propensity to violence'.

The judge announced that she would like to bring the first day of the trial to a close, but our lawyer asked her to hear another expert witness. I was surprised; this wasn't something we had discussed. The judge didn't seem too pleased to be taken off guard in this way either. Our lawyer said that he had been approached during the recess by a psychologist who had read of the trial in the papers and come to watch because he had known Tiberius. He had once been asked to write an assessment of him. Now the judge's attention was grabbed, and the prosecutor also agreed to hear the expert witness.

I was nervous at the prospect, because I felt the trial had gone well so far. My greatest worry, in particular, had not been realised: that people might see Dieter Tiberius as the victim in a confrontation between rich and poor, making us the wicked rich people who had disputed a poor man's right to his place in society. Now it looked as if the psychologist might head in that direction. He was wearing corduroy trousers gone baggy at the knees and a checked jacket with leather elbow patches. A pair of reading glasses dangled from his neck.

'Let's hear what you have to say, then,' said the judge, after the psychologist had taken his place in the witness stand and introduced himself. I leaned forward so as to hear him better. Beside me, Rebecca too seemed tense.

The psychologist had got to know Dieter Tiberius when he was twenty-eight. The social welfare office had sent him because he had been declared unfit for work owing to severe depression and they wanted to know if it was true.

'I conducted several interviews with him,' said the psychologist. 'Dieter Tiberius comes from a lower-middle-class family who were not truly poor but not wealthy either. His father abandoned the family early on—completely abandoned them. He had no further contact with his son, in spite of the boy's entreaties, and paid no alimony, although he later had a good position as a sales representative for a company that made electrical goods. Tiberius's mother couldn't manage to work and care for her son at the same time. She often hit him, and she locked him out of the house, at first for hours at a time, then for entire days, and once overnight. There were regular visits from social workers, until eventually the mother gave up and put her son into state care. He was nine years old at the time.'

In the children's home, the psychologist reported, Tiberius, who was fat even then, became the preferred victim of the other boys. His above-average intelligence also played a part—Tiberius was clever, said the psychologist. He described vividly and at length what Dieter Tiberius had gone through: humiliation, beatings, sexual abuse. Once he had been forced to brush his teeth with his own faeces. I confess that I did not feel pity listening to this report, but concern. I heard sighs, and wondered how the court would react to Dieter Tiberius's suffering.

When Tiberius was twenty, the psychologist continued, it looked as if he had managed to free himself from his troubled background. He caught up on his missed education, did an IT course and found a job he liked. But then, five years later, he resigned, and withdrew from society altogether. Dieter Tiberius had indeed been severely depressed, the psychologist said: the 'multiple traumas' of his childhood and adolescence had led to an extreme form of indolence. Could he tell the court what that was, the judge asked. 'Lethargy,' said the psychologist. 'Apathy.'

The prosecutor asked whether Dieter Tiberius had exhibited paedophilic tendencies. My wife took my hand. I think we both held our breath; we were about to discover

DIRK KURBJUWEIT

what threat we had really been exposed to. In the past I had
hoped it was a minor threat; now I hoped for a major one.
It was over; nothing could happen to us anymore. All that
mattered was that the shooting appear justified.

'Definitely not,' said the expert witness.

I was appalled. This man's testimony made it seem that
Dieter Tiberius had not deserved to die.

Had Tiberius been a violent person? asked the prosecutor.

'Definitely not,' said the expert witness again, with the
pleasure of a man who is able to say something surprising.
A murmur went through the crowd.

I couldn't believe it. It wasn't possible. He had done us
so much violence; we had suffered such a lot. And this man
was trying to tell us he hadn't been violently disposed? Our
justification of the shooting suddenly looked flimsy, even to
me. It wasn't that I doubted we bore some small measure of
blame for Dieter Tiberius's death, but I set it off against the
guilt I would have felt if anything had happened to my wife
and children. This argument was starting to seem specious.
My wife and children hadn't been under threat; I had only
assumed that they were. That, too, counts for something, but
assumption does not have the full moral force of reality.

My father's lawyer now intervened. He listed all that
Dieter Tiberius had done to us and ended with the words:
'That is the profile of a violent man.'

'On the contrary,' said the psychologist, 'Dieter Tiberius

had masochistic tendencies.' Again I heard a murmur go through the courtroom.

'Can you elaborate on that?' our lawyer asked.

'Certainly,' said the psychologist. 'Nothing aroused Dieter Tiberius more than angry women.'

At that moment I heard a scream such as I had never heard before and have never heard since. This scream seemed to pierce my right eardrum, for my wife was on my right and it was she who was screaming, shrilly, and without let-up, first sitting and then standing, as everybody stared. The judge asked what was wrong but got no answer; Rebecca had no words. The usher approached us to lead her out, but she wouldn't let him.

'Rebecca,' I said soothingly, 'sit down next to me.'

To my surprise, she stopped screaming as abruptly as she had started, and then sat down and listened, apathetically, as the psychologist went on.

'If I may permit myself a remark on the subject,' he said, 'I should like to. May I?'

'By all means,' said the judge.

'Tiberius,' the psychologist explained, 'staged the entire drama to send Mrs Tiefenthaler into a rage; he wanted to hear her scream because it aroused him. Is it possible to enrage a mother more than by accusing her of sexually abusing her children?'

The courtroom went quiet.

Rebecca had understood at once. I knew how she was feeling because I felt similar. Sullied, once again, and now abused as well. Dieter Tiberius had played a sly game with us and we'd been taken in. He knew how volatile Rebecca was; he had heard her screaming fits from the basement, and with his impudent remarks and accusations he had deliberately driven her into a frenzy.

'He raped me,' Rebecca said quietly to me. 'No, that's not it; he had sex with me and I was compliant.'

I took her in my arms, a betrayed husband of sorts, but one who couldn't be angry with his wife because she wasn't to blame for her betrayal. All about me I now saw sympathetic glances from the crowd. The mood in the courtroom had once again tipped in our favour.

The trial ended with no further incidents. The prosecutor didn't change his mind; on the second day of the hearing he asked for a verdict of murder. He recognised, he said, that my father had wanted to protect his family from danger, but in planning the unlawful killing of another man, he had knowingly committed the most brutal act of vigilante justice imaginable. My father had not been directly affected by the stalking, the prosecutor noted, and other possible solutions to the problem, such as relocating my family, had not been considered.

The defining characteristic of a murder, malice aforethought, was met, he said, because the victim had been unsuspecting and defenceless; he hadn't reckoned with such an attack from the accused, couldn't have reckoned with it and, what is more, had no appropriate means of defence or realistic means of escape. The prosecutor concluded by saying that the law left him no choice but to demand life imprisonment, even if that did mean that the accused would be released in fifteen years at the earliest. Given his age, this sentence was particularly severe—but unavoidably so.

Our lawyer pleaded for a verdict of manslaughter and a sentence of six years. He put particular stress on the family's predicament; I needn't go into the arguments again. The court concurred with our view and ruled manslaughter, but added two years to the sentence requested by the defence: eight years, release after four years at the earliest, day release after one to two years if the penal system agrees. We are awaiting that agreement now.

34

'DAD?'

I was there again today. My father didn't answer, sat there half asleep again. The children were with me; once a month I take them along. To begin with, we were in a fortnightly rhythm, but it's hard in prison with children. At first they cried because they thought that the heavy barred doors that closed behind them would never open again. Over time, they became more sure of themselves and ran riot in the corridors. I told them to be quiet, until it occurred to me that there is actually no reason to be quiet in a prison. Then the boredom set in. They were bored today, too, although they had their drawing things with them. They shared the visitor's chair and drew landscapes with animals while I talked to Kottke. Sometimes they raised their heads to see what Grandad was doing. He sat there, deep down inside himself, and said nothing. He gives them the creeps. I noticed that a while ago, and I hope he hasn't noticed, I really do.

Kottke told me how highly regarded my father is in prison. The other inmates admire him because he did away with that 'bastard', in spite of his age. Kottke has told me this more than once, and I always take it to mean that the other inmates despise me because I left the dirty work to my father. Besides, I disapprove of such eulogies, because I don't know what effect it has on my children to hear that the criminals in prison regard their grandad as a hero. It's not what we've told the children. After the shooting, of course, we had to talk to them, and we told them that Grandad couldn't bear to see the harm being done to his family, so he decided to put an end to it, and that was quite understandable, although it was not, of course, right to shoot people. It is not so easy to explain such a complex matter to children. We also told them that it was fair that Grandad had been given a punishment—that he was sitting it out now, and afterwards he would be released and all would be well again. My children had questions of a practical nature, such as whether Grandad would be able to read his magazines in prison, and we were able to reassure them on that count. They now cope very well with having a grandad in prison, but they do moan before visits because they get so bored there.

It's harder for me, too, when they are with me, because the topic uppermost in Kottke's mind is crime, and he lacks any sense of what atrocities you can (or can't) expose children to, even though he has three children of his own. I had to steer him carefully around the topic again today, lead him on to more innocuous territory, and we talked for a while about coins, although that's not something that interests me. Kottke collects coins and has a lot to say on the subject.

The hour dragged on. Ten minutes before it was up, I told the children to pack up their drawing things. Fay had drawn a farm, grazing cows and, above it all, a sun behind bars. She got up, went round the table and gave the picture to her grandad. He thanked her. Paul gave him a racing car. He smiled. The children were embarrassed saying goodbye to their grandfather; they gave him their hands without looking at him. They gave Kottke their hands too, my father and I hugged, and then we went home.

35

THE FRONT GATE SQUEAKS; I look up. The Moldovan woman is coming home. She sees me looking and waves a hand. I wave back. Small neighbourly smiles on her face and mine. The Moldovan woman from the laundry now lives in the basement, a stout woman in her late thirties, a quiet, agreeable neighbour from whom we have nothing to fear. We did panic briefly when she baked us a cake once, afraid that it might be the start of some new horror, but it wasn't. She keeps herself to herself, with only occasional displays of goodwill towards us, and in return we give her small presents that might come in useful: a thermos flask, some pretty salad servers. She doesn't have much money.

Sometimes the laundry manager comes round in the evening and stays for an hour or two. He lives nearby with his family, but we've no bourgeois hang-ups; let people do what they like, as long as they can square it with themselves. We turn the music up a bit, Mahler's second and fifth symphonies at the moment. When we meet the laundry manager at the front gate, we don't smirk, although his raspberry-coloured cords invite it. He always wears raspberry-coloured cords when he visits the Moldovan woman. There's a shop in Charlottenburg with a wide range of coloured cords on sale for men. I wonder why a certain type of man—over fifty, usually bald—feels the need to sheathe his legs in coloured corduroy.

My Black Print is almost gone. I have drunk a lot while writing today, because what is coming is not easy for me. I have to put down the words that haven't yet been said, so that I can, perhaps, say them at last, to Rebecca, to Bruno, to my mother, and some day to the children. They, I think, are the ones who should be told, but I shy from telling them, because I am afraid they will see me with different eyes—maybe disown me, maybe admire me, I don't know. Anything is possible, but I'd prefer it if everything stayed the way it is. We have found our way back to normality, a new normality, a post-Tiberius normality, to put it pretentiously.

If we didn't go to visit my father regularly, our day-to-day life would be similar to what it used to be—although, it's true, I suppose, that I still patrol the garden at night, not because I believe the ghost of Dieter Tiberius might come back to haunt us, but because I can't shake off the fear that he might have had a friend, another of his own kind, who is plotting to avenge his lost companion. I take the dog with me; he has to go out at night anyway. He sniffs and snorts; once or twice I have caught him staring in bewilderment at a hedgehog. The fox, which we know is there, eludes us; we have never seen another person either. Most likely there is no avenger, but we will never feel as safe as we used to. That does not, however, mean I have a gun.

What we do have is our Rhodesian ridgeback, big and broad; gentle at home, but dangerous on the street and even more so immediately outside the house. When I take him for a walk, I sometimes think I've ended up like my father: I am armed. Benno is not a killer, not bloodthirsty; we haven't trained him to attack. But his natural aggressiveness is enough to get me into a lot of awkward situations. I have to mollify people when he barks at them, or jumps up at them in spite of his lead. At home I snuggle up to him on the floor and we both like that, but he does detract rather from my claim to enlightened middle-class values. Anyone walking around with an enormous beast like that seems antisocial. But we need Benno; Rebecca would never have regained her equilibrium without him. When all was well again and Dieter Tiberius no longer able to harm us, my wife's spirits had darkened. Rebecca, who had borne so much, so bravely, all through the crisis, and been so sensible and level-headed, now cried a lot, without being able to say why. Things didn't improve until the dog came to live with us. He gives Rebecca the sense of security she needs.

Our marriage has essentially remained what it became thanks to Dieter Tiberius. That's a harsh thing to say, I know, but sometimes it does us good to say things that hurt—all the more so if they're true. When Dieter Tiberius set about destroying our family, it was more or less destroyed already. That is also too harsh. Why does pain sometimes do us such good? I don't know; I only feel it. If I look at the history of my marriage with cool detachment, it is clear to me that it was in a state of severe crisis when Dieter Tiberius entered our lives, and that it was he who enabled me to take an honest look at myself, my wife and our marriage. After that, things improved.

Thank you, Dieter Tiberius.

Now that really hurts. But sometimes the toads, those warty guardians of my unconscious, allow those words to rise up. I wave the thanks away, banish them to the depths of the well, regarding these expressions of gratitude as unwarranted, but I can't pretend not to notice that they occasionally surface. If only we really were the masters of our thoughts. But at least I can say that nothing makes me happier than to be with my wife—that I have not once relapsed into my old self-sufficiency, and now live and think and feel as if I were not complete without Rebecca. That, I think, is probably the best basis for a marriage. I'm not talking about a symbiosis; we remain autonomous beings—it is only that we are incomplete autonomous beings without one another.

I am afraid, though, that I am not always sure my wife feels the same way. I have noticed that in a certain situation she is very quick to give in to the dog. Our Rhodesian ridgeback is jealous, and whenever I hug Rebecca, he immediately thrusts himself between us. I would drive him away, but my wife lets him push us apart. A trivial thing, I know, but it is accompanied by a slight reserve that is new in her. Maybe her terrible memories are to blame, or maybe it's me. Does she, like my brother, like the prison inmates, think me a coward?

All in all, though, I would maintain that the crisis brought out the best in my family. We stood the test. We were threatened, but we stuck together, showing ourselves capable of defending ourselves, and emerging victorious—although 'victorious' might not be the right word. We combined our efforts and secured our safety. Can anything better be said of a family? I don't think so.

And I have a father again. I shall leave that statement as it stands, without further comments.

We have taken care of my mother. I have rented her a

small flat not far from us, a very pretty flat, overlooking a garden. The landlord doesn't mind my mother making herself useful in the garden, and she loves that—cutting roses or watering the tomatoes. Almost every day she comes to see us and plays with the children or reads to them. She misses her husband, to be sure, but her new life isn't all that bad, especially as I am, of course, once again able to furnish her with stories about my happiness and success. I've sorted things out with my little brother, too, and we are friends again. Sometimes my voice wobbles when I have to make a speech, but I can live with that.

I often ask myself whether it was right to put an end to Dieter Tiberius's life. It is not a matter I treat lightly; such thoughts torment me. He never attacked us, and we could probably have gone on living with him for ever, waiting for the day when he'd had enough of my wife's fits of anger. But would he ever have had enough? And what kind of life would that have been? We would have lived in constant fear, because we'd never have found out what game Dieter Tiberius was playing with my wife. At the end of such broodings, I never say to myself it was right, or it was wrong. Dieter Tiberius's death weighs on my conscience, although I could not imagine continuing to live under the same roof as him. What troubles me more than anything is that he only ever attacked us with words, never with deeds; that he violated our minds, not our bodies; that he used a sophisticated cultural tool—the poem—albeit in a deplorable form, to attack my family. We were the barbarians in the end. But I'm rambling. I shouldn't ramble. I should get round to putting down what I have to say. I have just opened another bottle of Black Print and taken a big gulp. Blue teeth—I'll have blue teeth now. I know that without having to look in the mirror. My gaze wanders out to the gas lamp, as if I were hoping to find solace or strength in its glow, to face what is to come. When I look at that street lamp I almost always think of a poem by Alexander Blok.

> Night, pavement, street lamp, chemist's shop,
> A pointless, dimly glowing light.
> Keep on another twenty years—
> Things stay the same. There's no way out.
>
> You die—you start over again.
> And this time too, it's all the same:
> Night, icy ripples on the canal,
> Chemist's shop, pavement, dim street lamp.

Isn't that the way it is? First I'm afraid that my father is going to climb the stairs and attack me, then I'm afraid that Dieter Tiberius is going to climb the stairs and attack us. My life begins with the fear of weapons, I do everything to escape that fear, but then I give in to it, and a man is shot.

Stop! Stop and speak the truth at last.

36

THE TRUTH. On the morning of the third day of his visit, my father was sitting in our kitchen, a pistol on the table in front of him, a Walther PPK. I joined him, and at first we acted as if there was no pistol lying there between us. We drank coffee and sat in silence. After a while, my father pushed the Walther PPK across to me, and there it lay beside my espresso cup. I looked at my father, and he gave me a nod. I didn't think about it for long; I took the gun and went down the stairs to the basement, to the door of Dieter Tiberius's flat.

All this time I held the pistol in my right hand, not stiffly or at arm's length, but in the way of one who does something familiar, something natural. The wooden grip fitted snugly into my hand. I don't remember thinking anything. I had a pistol in my hand and I was going to shoot Dieter Tiberius. There was no doubt, no pause for thought. I was will, not reason.

When I rang the bell, it wasn't long before Dieter Tiberius opened the door. Usually he laid low and didn't answer, but that was after we'd come clattering or screaming down the stairs. This time I'd been quiet; he couldn't know who was standing outside his flat. I heard his footsteps. A chain was drawn back, then the door was flung open. I raised my arm and shot Dieter Tiberius in the head. He was standing a metre and a half from me, and I wouldn't be my father's son if I missed a target at that distance. I turned around and went back upstairs.

My father was standing in the doorway. He took the gun from me and carried it into the kitchen, where he cleaned it carefully with one of his polishing cloths so that only his fingerprints would be found on it later in the laboratory. When he had finished, he said, 'You should ring the police now.' I did as I was told and rang the police. 'Wash your hands,' my father said then, and again, I obeyed.

It took eight minutes for the police to arrive.

'I have shot the basement tenant,' my father said to

Sergeant Leidinger. That was a lie.

I, Randolph Tiefenthaler, shot the basement tenant. That is the truth.

37

IF I REMEMBER RIGHTLY, in the days that followed I barely thought about the fact that I was now a murderer. There was so much commotion, and all the commotion revolved around my father having killed Dieter Tiberius, so that I took on the role that implied: the man whose father had killed Dieter Tiberius. We had several talks with our lawyer, visited my father in custody, and took care of my mother. We took care of the children too, of course, so that they weren't wrenched out of their happy childhood by their grandfather's crime—their grandfather's *alleged* crime, I should say, can say, now that the truth is out at last. I was in a trance, so caught up in my role that I really believed it. I was the man whose father had killed Dieter Tiberius. Because everyone acted as if that was the truth, I accepted it as the truth.

That worked up to a point—until one evening when I was at Hedin with my wife. It was three weeks after the murder. I hadn't been to a starred restaurant alone since my nosebleed, and it had never occurred to us to go together, perhaps because such places were a reminder of darker times of our marriage. But after three weeks, I said to Rebecca, 'Let's go to Hedin. Let's have a nice evening out.' The commotion had died down; we could see that my father was coping well with his life in custody; that my mother, although sometimes distressed, was not going to pieces; and that our children, after their initial bewilderment, were once more living and playing cheerfully.

I booked a table, my mother came around to babysit, and then there we were, in that coolly metropolitan room: blue chairs, finely grained wood, Chinese vases in lime green, a big Harald Hermann picture of plump bin bags bulging out of rubbish bins. In this day and age, in my circles, everything has to be ironically undermined. We see exquisite things even in rubbish—an aestheticised rubbish, of course. If pictures exuded the smell of the things they depict, that Hermann would not be hanging in Hedin.

Rebecca and I began our dinner without champagne. We hadn't talked about it, but we had a tacit understanding that there would be nothing celebratory about the evening. We were glad to be rid of Dieter Tiberius, but we didn't think a man's death cause for rejoicing. I ordered a low-priced red wine and we drank in moderation, talking about the children and my wife's desire to go back to working in research. After the third course, langoustines with Greenland salt and celeriac puree, I suddenly felt uneasy, and broke into a sweat.

'What's wrong?' Rebecca asked, seeing my light blue shirt turn dark.

'I don't know,' I said, but I already had a suspicion. The other diners were there to enjoy themselves, and although the people who sit in Hedin may like watching plays where people get murdered, or arguing about murderous regimes in Africa and Asia, or calling the government of the United States a murderous regime, they do not want to spend their evenings in the presence of a murderer—only, perhaps, at the very most, a murderer who has served his sentence and been rehabilitated. That might be just about acceptable, but it didn't apply to me. I could sense them sensing that I was a murderer and knew I was encroaching upon their enjoyment of the evening, tainting the atmosphere. Today I can see that it was all in my head, but at the time I couldn't. I suddenly felt hugely present, hugely visible, as I never had before; I'd never wanted to attract attention, be in the limelight, make speeches. I was happy to be inconspicuous.

We left before dessert, chocolate from French Guiana in a maize crust.

The next day I had a similar attack in a coffee shop where I had planned to drink a quick espresso. Nothing is spreading in Berlin as fast as these coffee shops—chains like Starbucks and so on—where everyone goes for instant revival and to fortify themselves against the coming hour. This city is nervous in the extreme—hypersensitive. Everyone is so overloaded with impressions and noises and confrontations of every kind that even a little extra pushes them over the edge, into neurasthenia, as it used to be called. I was now that little extra, I thought, the murderer, whose presence was the final imposition, too much to bear.

Nor could I find respite in my work. I, of all people, built houses for a living, homes in which to live a peaceful life—and who could ever be at peace in a house built by a murderer?

38

I COULDN'T STAND BERLIN ANYMORE, because Berlin could no longer stand me, or so I believed, and I told Rebecca I needed some time out, a week of peace and relaxation, away from it all. She could well understand: I was, she thought, the son of a murderer and had a lot to come to terms with. I flew to Bolzano, a town in the Italian Alps, and from there took a taxi to a remote guesthouse. I'm not a hiker, I'm not a mountain person, but I had once been to a conference in Bolzano and liked the starkness of the Dolomites. Even a murderer could not disturb the equanimity of mountains like these, which have been around for millions of years.

I moved into my room at midday and set off in the early afternoon with no plan, no aim. I took the path that led past the guesthouse, following it uphill. I had barely taken the first few steps before I was beset by the questions I had so far kept at bay. How could someone who hated guns shoot a man dead? How could someone who set such store by the rule of law take the law into his own hands?

My first thought was that we'd been living in a bubble. We had panicked, and our panic had cut us off from reality, from reason, from our better selves. We had retreated into a bubble and lived our panicked lives there. Children make you vulnerable to this kind of thinking; you tell yourself you'll do anything to protect your family without asking what that means.

It was from within this bubble that I began to plan the murder, I thought, as I made my way up the mountainside. I planned the murder, but somebody else, my father, would be carrying it out, and that made it easier, perhaps—extenuated the moral issue somewhat. It also, to be sure, raised another moral issue. I was using my father's skill to my own purposes, yet as his son I felt justified in doing so. If I ended up as the gunman, it was because of the situation, the emotional charge. My father pushed the pistol across to me, and I was so astonished that I thought no more, but only acted.

Now I was angry with him, angry with him for dragging me into it, but not for long; after only a few more steps I realised that it was in fact I who had dragged him into it, that he had followed my plan—apart from not wanting to be the gunman, choosing instead merely to pass as the gunman. He had every right. Doesn't it make Dad's sacrifice even greater, that he accepted life in prison for a crime he hadn't committed? For me.

I pushed on for about an hour, caught up in these thoughts. Ahead of me, the peaks of Santner and Euringer pierced the sky, sheer and angry. There were no longer any trees, only grass and scree. I was sweating profusely. It was already growing dark, but I kept walking. I was feeling good, in spite of the troubling thoughts that kept surfacing; the massif could cope with them, and it could cope with me. It was all right for me to be here, though I was guilty of murder, or manslaughter, to be precise, not that it made much difference; it didn't matter to me how long the sentence was.

I marched on up the mountain, a law-abiding man who had broken the law. And yet the law is absolute. It admits no exception. That should be obvious, but it was only now that I was trying to find myself a loophole that I realised it. There is no loophole. The law must be merciless, its rule totalitarian. Any exception destroys it. It does not, however, ostracise a criminal forever; it punishes him, and once his punishment is served, the criminal is exonerated. But that path is not open to me, because I'm not facing up to my punishment, not taking responsibility: there will be no relief, only cruel, shameful guilt going on forever.

I was thinking this when I realised that it was almost dark. This was a shock. I was suddenly afraid of the mountains, but the next moment I didn't care, and when I realised that things weren't looking all that bad, I was even disappointed: I'd been charging up the mountain in a straight line, never turning right or left, so it would be easy to find my way back to the guesthouse. I turned around and walked down the mountain through the darkness. Several times I stumbled, because I was exhausted and because I wasn't wearing hiking boots, only running shoes, which didn't have enough grip. I ended up with bruises, and a scratch on my face, and I felt like an idiot for having timed this walk so badly and set out so ill-equipped, but my life was in no danger and part of me thought that a shame. I reached the guesthouse in safety but was so exhausted that I lay down on the bed fully clothed and immediately fell asleep.

In the mirror the next morning, I saw grazes on my right cheek, fine lines scabbed over red. The face of a murderer, I thought—but why should a murderer look like that? I took the bus into a nearby town and bought myself hiking boots, map, knife, rucksack, lunch box and torch, and a fleece jacket, too, because it was colder than I had expected. At midday I set off again. A desolate sky swelled above me;

tattered clouds, grey and blue and dark grey, chased across it, wild and turbulent. I thought largely about the same things as yesterday. In the evening I sat alone in the snug; I was the only guest. An old woman brought me home-cooked food and bottled beer. The furniture was made of a wood that was almost black. On one wall hung a crucifix, on another a round plaque cut from a tree trunk, with folksy handpainted lettering. *Every good gift is from above*, it said. A green-tiled stove was roaring in the corner. When I sat next to it, it wasn't long before I began to sweat, but as soon as I moved away I felt the cold. So I moved back and forth, and tried to concentrate on a novel. When the old woman took my plate, she didn't say a word, and that was fine by me.

Because I was awake at five the following day, I went to the cowshed and watched the old woman and her husband milking the cows. After breakfast I set off again. I thought of turning myself in, accepting the punishment I deserved and atoning. But what would be gained? My children would lose their father, my wife her husband, and all three would be left without support. They would have to sell the flat and might still be in debt even then. And there was no guarantee that my father would be released. He had supplied the murder weapon and was an accomplice; he wouldn't get off without punishment. I would, it was true, be able to atone at last for the crime I had committed, but in my situation that would be selfish. It might ease my conscience, but it would harm my family—and my father is where he is today because he sees everything the way I do. The rubber soles of my boots crunched on the scree. I could hear my breathing—nothing else. There was a light rain. I felt all right, up there in the mountains.

Every day I continued to walk through the autumn landscape. I left my phone at the guesthouse and listened to my voicemail when I returned in the late afternoon. A few business calls and, without fail, my wife and children. On the second or third day, I stopped returning business calls, and then I stopped calling my family back. I watched the milking in the cowshed every morning; I would have liked to help, but the old people turned down my offer. As soon as it got light, I set off into the mountains, whatever the weather. I walked briskly, didn't meet a soul, and when I was hungry I sat down on a log to eat my lunch. I chewed smoked sausages, ate a roll, drank some milk and went on my way.

My thoughts often touched on Dieter Tiberius. I had hoped that the murder—the manslaughter—would do away with him, but now his ghost was breathing down my neck. I compared his life with mine, compared our fathers, who had presumably made all the difference. His had left and mine had stayed—eccentric, but present. Staying is a big deal, I thought, because leaving is a big deal. I swore there and then never to leave my own family, but the virtuous feeling it gave me was yet another instance of my smug self-satisfaction, my cheap complacency.

I wondered, too, whether I had ended up shooting because of the home I came from, because shooting was something I was more or less born with.

'You see, it *is* your genes,' Rebecca would say.

'No,' I would reply. 'It's not my genes. My father never shot anyone. He doesn't have it in him. He's not a murderer. He can't—won't. He's harmless. It was me,' I would continue. 'I had the choice and it was my decision.'

But I had stopped speaking to Rebecca. Every afternoon I lay on the bed, which was too short for me, and brooded—and if the phone rang I looked at the display to see who it was, but I didn't answer. I put it on mute, fell asleep, woke up and saw the vibrating phone working its way across the bedside table. I sat up, saw that it was Rebecca and lay down again. The phone was dragging itself towards the edge like a wounded animal. I wanted to pick it up, but I felt paralysed. If I took hold of it, I would have to speak into it, but I couldn't say what I had to say. It fell to the floor. I heard it buzz twice more, then there was quiet. I lay in bed until suppertime. Could I stay longer than the week I had originally planned? I asked the old woman that evening. No trouble at all, she said.

The weather worsened: gales, the first snow. I went out every day all the same, even if only for an hour. The rest of the time I lay in bed or hung around the yard and the cowshed. When I got back from walking on the tenth day, Rebecca was sitting in the snug.

'Randolphrandolphrandolph,' she said, 'I know you're in a bad way, but we need you at home.'

The next day I flew back to Berlin with her. I was a little frightened that I would again begin to feel I couldn't impose myself on this overwrought city, but it didn't happen. I coped tolerably well for the first few days, and after that Berlin was once again my city. Normality set in, post-Tiberius normality.

But the words I have to say are still missing. I am ready. I just haven't decided yet whether to give Rebecca this account or to talk to her some time, when we're out walking the dog, perhaps. I suppose it doesn't make much difference. What matters is that she soon finds out who it is she is living with. I have thought of combining the news, which might come as a shock to my wife, with some other, more pleasant announcement. I'll tell her that I am almost ready to design and build a home for my family. She would like a house, and I will make her wish come true.

ACKNOWLEDGMENTS

I should like to thank Thomas Ante and Friedhelm Haas.

The menus in this book come from Berlin restaurants Tim Raue, Reinstoff and Vau.

Let us know if you've been

#GrippedByFear

Leave a review online and tweet us @orionbooks
to discuss the book with other readers